True Diamond Publications Presents

Trifling 3

By

Jennifer Luckett

Copyright 2014 by Jennifer Luckett Trifling 3

All rights reserved. No part of this book may be reproduced in any form or by electronic or mechanical means, including information storage and retrieval systems without permission in writing from the publisher, except by a reviewer who may quote brief passages in review.
First Edition August 2014
Printed in the United States of America

This is a work of fiction. Names, characters, places, and incidents either are products of the author's imagination or are used fictitiously. Any similarity to actual events or locales or persons, living or dead, is entirely coincidental.

More Drama Going Down

Sparkle

I stood there in a state of shock with my right hand over my chest as the paramedics took Pops. They rushed him off to the hospital from Mama V's engagement party. My heart was going so fast that I thought it would jump from my chest. I leaned against the wall to get myself together, and that's when Ginger began talking out the side of her neck. She flicked her hair and stared me down. "I think you should leave the party. Since you and Sayveon are no longer dating, I don't feel that you should be here. Besides, he's mine now," she uttered and held her nose up in the air in a conceited way. Sayveon has this trick wide open and full of herself, I thought.

Ginger gave me a wide smile. Her eyes moved up and down my body before she rolled them, and then they landed right back on me. I shook my head because, I really wasn't up for the drama, but it seemed that she was gassed up and ready to start some shit. "I need a drink now from all of that commotion," she said and grabbed her drink that she was sipping on prior to the unexpected disturbance earlier. She took a few gulps and redirected her attention to me. "Why are you still standing there? Go home," she bossed.

"Keep poppin' shit and you gonna get yo' forehead tapped," I snapped off, warning her. "Unless you got hands, don't come over here with that."

I was letting her know that unless she was ready to fight don't step to this because she was about to be touched. I was tired of the silly bird- bitch.

"Whatever. You better not blink hard at me or I'll slap you."

I grabbed the hooker by the collar and slammed her into the wall. Ginger slipped down and fell on the floor. "Stop acting like you 'bout it hoe," I said while tagging that ass.

She ran up; now she was gettin' done up. I stuck her with my fists and started swinging blow after blow. My right hand grabbed her throat when she swung off. Her hands immediately went up to her neck. I reached out, grabbing a couple of good handfuls of hair, and pulled her toward me. I lifted my leg and rammed my knee into her gut.

"Aargh," she released, letting out a painful grunt and collapsed to her knees. Her left hand held her throat, and her right one was planted over her stomach. When she bent over, I noticed that her left tittie had come out. I made a few steps around to her left side and let the toe of my stiletto kick the dangling tit. Before I could finish her off, I felt two huge arms wrap around my waist, pick me up and carry me outside. Mama V's two cousins, Diego and his brother told me to stand outside and calm down.

A few minutes later Sayveon hung up his phone and moved my way. "What's going on? Why they bring you out here?" he asked.

"I just got into it with your li'l hoe, Ginger. She kept coming at me, so I gave her what she wanted and got all over that ass," I told him.

Sayveon looked at Mama V's cousins. "Y'all can go back in. I got her," he said.

The two men turned and left. Sayveon wrapped his arms around me. "I'm sorry for all of the bullshit that I've put you through. I ain't happy with none of these broads, and all I want is to have my family back. I miss you and Layla. I want to make things back right."

His words touched me, and my eyes watered because as much as I hated to admit it, I missed him. I wanted him to do better and be the man I needed him to be. I placed my hand on his back and gently rubbed up and down. I loved my child's father but was afraid to give him my heart again. I'd been hurt too many times, and the pain was too much for me to ever want to feel like that again.

Sayveon used his finger to lift my head. "I just got off the phone with Carmen. I told her what happened to Pops. I want you to go to the hospital with me." I nodded my head. "I'm wrong for all of the shit I put you through, okay?" he said, apologizing again.

"Okay," I said, accepting his apology. "I'll go up there with you, but what are you going to do with the two groupies you brought with you?"

He chuckled a bit. "I'll let them catch a taxi back if I have to. I'll handle that," he assured.

I smiled and turned to go back into the party to talk to Mama V before going up to the hospital. I stopped and pulled down my red mini-dress and ran my fingers through my bang. After readjusting my clothing and making sure my hair was straight, I went in. The DJ was playing the music again. I could hear it as soon as I opened the door to the huge ballroom where the party was going on. Mama V and several others were on the dance floor dancing to Otis Redding's old school tune, 'Sitting On The Dock Of The Bay.' I would have never expected a woman her age to have the energy and spunk to move the way she was moving. She was simply astounding. She boogied with the rhythm and agility of a person half her age. She danced circles around Mr. Travis. Ginger sang along to the tune, "Ooh, I'm sitting on the dock of the bay/wasting time..." Her hand went in the air as she smiled and carried on having fun.

I stepped to Mama V and leaned over in her ear. "Do it, girl."

"I just love to dance. This keeps me alive. Music brings happiness," she said back. She grabbed my hand and twirled me around in a circle, laughing. Mr. Travis caught my other hand, and we all laughed and giggled. Moving around with them made me feel better and showed me that Mama V had had enough of Pops because she was still enjoying her party. A few minutes passed before the song neared its end.

Sayveon stepped inside the door and walked over to Mr. Travis and told him he was about to leave. I watched him make his way over to the Chinese chick and handed her some money. I guessed it was so that she and Ginger could catch a cab back to Ginger's crib. While I was dancing, I cut my eyes over at him and saw him whisper something into Ginger's ear and then point over at the Chinese girl. He then got all up in her face, and I could tell he was snapping off on her. He said a few more words and then walked toward the door and gestured for me to come on. He was ready to bounce. Ginger slowly stepped her stupid ass over to where we were dancing and reached for Mama V's hand. Ginger swayed her hips to the tune. I could tell she was tipsy by the sound of her voice when she slurred, "C'mon let's get this party started."

"Get away from me you filthy heifer," Mama V mouthed and snatched away from her. Instead of Ginger getting the point, she stood right in front of Mr. Travis, leaned over, and bounced her ass. That dizzy broad had fucked up. Before I could knock her down, Mama V grabbed her by the arm and pushed her off her man. "Get this whore out of here," she ordered Sayveon.

Sayveon twisted his body back around, went over to Ginger, snatched her up by the arm, and made her go out of the door with him. I assumed that he'd changed his mind about the cab. I told Mama V that I'd see her later, and she nodded with a face full of frowns and patted me on the back. That clown ass hoe Ginger, had gotten on everybody's nerve. I walked away and followed the two out of the door. Once we got in the hall, I heard the click-clocking sound of another pair of shoes trailing behind us. I turned and noticed it was the Chinese broad following us. The front entrance door automatically opened wide, and we went outside into the chilly night air. Sayveon grabbed her around the neck and insulted her. "Dog ass bitch. You tryna embarrass me in front of my people?" he asked her.

She tried to pry his hands but was unsuccessful at her attempt. His grip must have grown tighter because her eyes started to waddle to the back of her head and her whole body trembled. He let her go and pushed her away from him. He held the back of his hand up, swung with full speed, and aimed for her cheek. Smack! He delivered a pimp slap that was loud enough to be heard throughout the city.

"Don't hit me like that," she whined holding the side of her jaw. She raised her dress and bent over. "Kiss my ass." Ginger slapped her butt cheek, let her clothing back down, and gave Sayveon the middle finger. "I'm tired of you treating me like shit whenever this slutbucket comes around!" She went off, referring to me by pointing her finger in my direction.

I reached over and whacked her finger. "Don't make me knock some sense into you," I cautioned and walked a few feet away to keep from banging her head into a wall.

"Sparkle," I heard Sayveon call out. I twisted my body around to face him. "I've decided to just go ahead and drop these two off. Jump in the car with me so I can take them back."

I frowned and waved him off. "I'll just go back into the building because I'm not gon' be riding around with you and these two pigeons. I can't deal, not like that," I objected, shaking my head from side to side.

"C'mon baby, ain't nobody gon' fuck with you." He slightly pulled my arm and walked me to his vehicle. "Get in the back Ginger and Jia," he told them.

Jia opened the backdoor and plopped down, but Ginger folded her arms. "Why does this whore get to sit up front and we have to get in the back? I hate her!"

"Look, I ain't gon' be too many more whores. You better check your tongue," I shot back.

She opened the back door and asked Jia, "Do you see anything on my tongue?" She licked her tongue out, and Jia shook her head no. She rose up and looked at me. "There's nothing wrong with my fucking tongue."

I knew right then that ole' girl was dumber than somebody building a house under water. I giggled a bit. I felt sorry for the blonde bimbo because she was the definition of the word 'slow.' While I stood there with a raised eyebrow, Sayveon quickly opened the door in the back, pushed her downward, and shoved her inside. "Sit yo' ass down," he barked.

"Ouch. You're hurting me." She lowered her head and pouted like a li'l kid would do when the parent tells them they can't have something. This shit was truly pitiful and stupid.

How in the world did I get myself tied into this mess? I asked myself. I opened the car door and got inside of the car. Sayveon leaned down in his seat and put one hand on the steering wheel. He turned the radio up and the sound of 'Work' by Meek Mill featuring Rick Ross flowed through the speakers as he pulled out of the parking lot. It was a quiet ride except for the music playing in the background.

We drove into The Briars Apartments in North Jackson and pulled into an empty parking spot beside Ginger's silver Acura RL. "Aight, I'll holla at y'all later. I'm headed to check on Pops," Sayveon said over his shoulder.

Jia got out. I heard Ginger open her door, and suddenly, I felt a strong force pulling the hell out of my hair, snatching my head back. "Shit!" I screamed out from the top of my voice and squirmed in the seat. "Let my mothafuckin' hair goooo!"

Sayveon put the car in park and hopped out. "Let her shit go," he bossed.

Slowly I could feel the pain easing up. Finally, he got her to let go. By now, my blood was boiling because this was the shit that I had gotten rid of. I hadn't been dealing with the different broads in the streets and all of the chaos that came along with having a d-boy as my man. With a balled fist, I slid from the passenger seat and stepped out of the vehicle. I took off my stiletto ankle boots and tossed them to the side of the car. I wrapped Ginger over her left eye and started giving her the business. "I'm...bout...sick...and... tired ...of ...you," I said while I popped that ass in the face. "How many times I got to beat you down before you learn, hoe?"

"Tear a hole in her ass," Sayveon advised. "She ought to keep her hands to herself." I got the chance to box her some more before he got in between us. He grabbed her and slapped her in the mouth a few times before making her go inside her crib. Jia trailed behind her, and the apartment door closed. It seemed that the dust had settled. You would have thought Sayveon had 14-carat gold balls and a magic wand for a dick by the way hoes sweat him so hard.

Sayveon and I had gotten inside of his whip and he was backing up when we I saw a huge object flying toward the windshield. Ginger was standing there looking deranged. Her chest heaved up and down and tears streamed from her eyes. Something crashed into the window. I noticed an object lying on top of the car and a crack in the window. The dummy had actually thrown a chair. My mouth flew open and I knew she should have started running when Sayveon reached under the seat, grabbed his nine milli, and hopped out of the car. From the expression on his face, I knew that 'nig' was 'bout to do some extra stupid goon shit to that trick.

Shit Is About To Get Real

Sayveon

My blood boiled, and I knew I had to show Ginger my getdown. I was the wrong nigga for her to play wit'. Wit' my hand gripping my burner, I mobbed back toward Ginger's crib. She had her hand on her hip talking shit, but she must have seen the rage in my eyes because she flew back inside and quickly shut the door behind her. I added some speed to my steps and ended up standing in front of her pad. I pounded on the front entrance. "Bitch, open up this goddamn door. Me and you 'bout to have some real problems!" I yelled. At that point, I was zoned out and 'bout to go into killa mode. I checked my surroundings and then kicked the door just below the doorknob. I felt it bend inward a bit. I kicked it again in the exact same spot. A few more kicks later, the door's frame splintered, and I was able to kick it loose.

I ran up in the spot and brushed pass Jia who was in the doorway. "Please, just leave her alone and let it go," she pleaded and grabbed at my arm. I snatched away from her.

"Where she at?" I got no response, so I continued to the bedroom. I didn't see her nowhere in sight. I moved to the closet and opened up the door, but she wasn't in there. I bent over and looked under the bed. Ginger was under the bed shaking, and her eyes bucked when she saw my face.

"I'm sorry," she apologized with a trembling voice, but I wasn't tryna hear that. I got a hold of one of her legs and dragged her from under there. "I won't do it again; Daddy just don't hurt me!" I ignored the loud cries.

"You got me fucked up."

I held up the butt of the heater and rapped her in the head. She collapsed down to the floor letting off the sound of a loud thump. With no remorse, I dotted the door and did jet time down the street headed to my destination.

I bust a right at the light, turned on North State Street, and parked under the parking garage of The Mississippi Baptist Hospital. Sparkle and I got out and walked inside the building toward the Emergency Room. We stopped at the station in the front. A young Caucasian girl who looked to be in her early twenties with a freckled face and red hair sat at the desk. She was on the phone, and she finished her conversation before she hung up, looked at us and asked, "Can I help you with something?"

"Yeah, I'm here to find out about my father named Al Rodriguez," I said. "He was brought here by the ambulance."

"Okay. Let me look in the computer, and I'll be able to give you some information on him." She glanced up. "What's his name again?"

"Al Rodriguez." I rubbed my hand down my sideburn and sighed.

"He's in the back. I'll unlock the door and let you go in there. When you get to the nurses' desk let them know who you're here to see, and they'll direct you to his room."

Sparkle thanked her, held my hand, and we both went on to the back. I told the nurse that I needed to see Pops and gave his name. The older black woman in her late fifties reminded me of my mother. With her soft-spoken tone and compassionate attitude, she led us across the hallway and pulled the curtain back.

"Mr. Rodriguez, your son is here to see you," she spoke in a caring and gentle way and patted him lightly on the shoulder. She looked at me. "We're about to run some tests on him to see if we can find out what the problem is. He's been complaining of chest and abdominal pain, and he's very nauseated."

I nodded and stepped over to see Pops. He was groaning on a gurney with a thin oxygen tube tucked beneath his nose. "We placed an IV in for hydration and pain relief. The tube will help with his breathing," the nurse informed me. I read her nametag that read, Angelica.

Again, I nodded. "Whatever y'all have to do to make sure he's gonna be alright, I'm wit' it."

I planted my hand on his leg. "You better pull through this old man," I tried to encourage him. He slowly opened his eyes and stared up at the ceiling for a minute before re-shutting his eyelids. Angelica told us that an EKG would be done and then he'd be wheeled down to have some x-rays taken. I let her know that I was going down to the waiting area. I left out of the room. It was killing me to see him looking like that. My whole life, I somewhat saw Pops as invincible. No matter what went on, he maintained and kept his head up. Now, he was fighting to survive. Sparkle trailed behind until we got to the waiting room where I sat and waited to hear the results about my old man's health. For the first time in months, I dropped my head and started to pray to the headman in charge. I knew without a doubt that he'd hear me in spite of my street status.

I silently prayed, *Lord I chose this life, but I kno' it ain't right. I'm out here tryna make it, and I ain't saying what I'm doing is good, 'cause it's wrong. Please, forgive me for my wrongs, and I need you to have some compassion on my life. My mom says having faith is what will bring blessings. I find it hard to pray because I can't see you, but I'm supposed to believe that you're here. Where were you when Rich got murked, and it was all over a bitch? Why you didn't come find me when a mothafucka burned my house down and blew my car up?*

A deep baritone voice that was so real said, "Let me stop you right here. Son, the biggest leap of faith believes that there is a higher power. Not only am I real, I'm everywhere. Water has no color, and you can see straight through it, yet you feel it and cannot live without it. Exodus 33:20 reads, But He said, 'you cannot see my face, for no man can see me and live.'

I was mute. I quietly said in my head, *God, I'm not trying to disrespect you in no kind of way. I only spoke my mind. If I didn't tell you how I felt, then I wouldn't be keepin' it real, and I ain't no phony nigga who gonna hide my thoughts. For all the bad that I've done, I apologize. From this day forward, I'll try to do my best. I ain't saying I won't ever fuck up. Can you make shit right, watch over my Pops, and give him the strength to get well and not leave me in this cold world? I need you right now.*

The Lord stated, "My will shall be done. Just remain strong through it all." The sound of his voice slowly vanished.

Sparkle's hand rubbed up and down my arm. "Are you okay?" she asked.

"I'm good." She got her phone from her small purse and started showing me pictures of our baby girl. Layla had grown, and I missed out on some of that. I regretted the way I treated 'Spark.' I looked deep into her eyes. "I need you. I'ma make shit better."

She smiled. "I will think about it, but I've heard all of this before. Why should I believe you now?"

Before I could respond I heard, "Hi, Sayveon. I just checked on Dad. He wasn't in the room, but I did talk to the nurse, and she gave me the latest details. They had taken him out for tests." Carmen hugged me around my neck before she took a seat right next to me. She wore a pair of gray skinny jeans, a white snugged fit long sleeve shirt, and on her feet were white and gray J's. Her long black hair was back and worn in a ponytail. Her thin face had been a sign that she lost weight. "Hi, Sparkle," she greeted.

Sparkle rolled her eyes and turned her lip up. I tried to downplay what my baby's momma did. "So, how you been doing?" I questioned Carmen.

"I'm gonna be okay." Carmen then wiped a tear from her eye. "I've already lost my mother. I don't want to lose someone else that's close to me. This is too much and I don't know how much more I can take." She sniffled.

I put my hand on her shoulder. "You gon' be a'ight. You gotta be strong and fight your way through all of this bullshit."

After a few minutes passed, all three of us got up and walked toward the room where Pops was. Angelica stopped us in the hall with a doctor beside her. "I'm Doctor James Wages. We've just found out through the abdominal x-ray that your father has some intestinal obstruction which means there is partial blockage of the bowel. I'm waiting for the chest x-ray to come back, but in the meantime I would like to go ahead and have a CAT scan performed."

"Go on and do what you need to do," Carmen said. "Is it alright if we go in and see him for a minute?"

"Sure." He moved out of the way and went on to another patient's room.

We all stepped in. "I'm giving him the liquids he needs to drink in order to take the CT scan," Angelica made known as she stood in front of Pops helping him to hold on to the first of two big containers of contrast liquids. He finished it, and his breathing grew phlegmy and labored. A black female geriatrician arrived and urged the insertion of a nasogastric tube to suck out all the liquid he had just downed. His blood oxygen levels dropped, and two doctors rushed in. The doctors and two nurses suctioned his throat until he gagged and then fastened an oxygen mask over his nose and mouth.

At one point, I looked at my sick father, still in pain despite all the apparatus, and thought, This is what suffering looks like. His skin was pale, and he appeared to be weak.

"I'm just so tired," Pops managed to slowly tell us. "There are too many things going wrong."

Carmen held on to Pops hand. He was ill, and I could see it in his eyes that he was tired of fighting that battle. He held his head back and rested his eyes. It hurt because there was nothing I could do to help the man who always looked out for me. All I could do was hope that he'd be alright. He was from the streets, so I knew he was a fighter.

When the staff asked us to step out so that they could work on him, we left out. As we stood outside the door, Carmen looked at me with a serious look. "We're going to have to discuss some things concerning Dad. Can I speak to you in private?" she asked.

I glanced over at Sparkle. "Baby, I'm about to step outside and talk to her." I kissed her on the forehead and gave her a hug.

"I'll be right here when you get back," she said.

Carmen and I went out of the door and stood outside of the Emergency Room. "What's up, shawdy?"

She dropped her head and from the way she was acting, I knew something was wrong. "Dad is really sick. I'm not even sure if he's able to keep dealing with all of these health issues."

"He's a G. He'll make it," I tried to convince her even though I was unsure if he would.

"I'm ready to go back home. I don't like being here. So many bad things have happened since I've moved to this state. And, my grandmother's health is failing. I think my mother's death is really taking its toll on her, and plus she's down there with my li'l sister. I need to help to raise my sister. My grandmother is aging, and I don't want to put that burden on her." She rubbed her teary eyes. "There are a lot of people in my family who think that my father had my mom and Rich killed. I don't want to believe that he'd do something like that."

I was silent and stood there looking up at the sky at a medical helicopter that was about to land on top of the building. I watched the chopper lower itself until it made its landing on the roof.

I wasn't gon' snitch our old man out. I guess he did what he felt he had to do when it came to Jackie and Rich. He loved her and had a lot of respect for Rich but once they betrayed him, he snapped and had them bodied.

"My time is up here. I'm going to be going back home next week. I want you to take care of Dad. He trusts you, and I'm not going to be able to see about Valencia and Grandma if I choose to stay here. They need me." She folded her arms across her chest and rubbed her arms. "I'm so stressed. I've lost about twenty pounds since I buried my mother."

"I'll watch out for him, don't worry. Go and take care of what you need to, and if I need you, I'll call. I'm sorry about you losing Veronica. Me and Rich were tight and shit ain't been the same since he's been gone." I took a deep breath and slowly let it out.

"Thanks and yes I know he was your buddy."

"Man, I'm sorry too for getting you preggos. I was out of order for touching you, but I didn't kno' you were my fam." I turned my head and looked away. Just speaking up on that shit made me feel some type of way; I hated to think about it. Dayum!

"It's over. Same here, I didn't know you were my brother. I shouldn't have come on to you. You're my family, and I love you big brother." She hugged my neck.

"Love you too li'l sis." She let go, opened up her tiny handbag, and pulled out a cigarette and lighter. She flicked the lighter and lit it. She placed her lips around the end of the cigarette and took a long drag.

I chuckled. "When did you start smoking, girl?"

"I just started about a week ago. It's the only thing that helps to calm my nerves," she said and blew a cloud of smoke in the air.

I heard footsteps coming our way and held my head up. A tall framed dude was coming toward me. When I noticed who the lame was, I waited for him to fuck up and step to me with some bogus bullshit. I didn't have my heat on my waistline. If he got wrong, we'd have to scrap it out.

Earlier That Day

Stephanie

On that day, I felt something inside of me, like a sense of loneliness. Every time I thought about James, I got sad. As I lay on the sofa, I heard a voice tell me to go visit his grave. I needed to get some things off my chest. I never had closure from this whole situation. It's like he just disappeared. I never had the opportunity to say goodbye. I lifted myself from the sofa, grabbed the remote from the glass center table, and turned the television off. As I put the remote down, I picked up my keys, locked up my apartment, and got in my car. I turned the radio up. Mariah Carey's throwback CD was playing the song, 'One Sweet Day' featuring Boyz To Men.

As I drove, I thought about all of the deadly situations I found myself in. God had mercy on me. He showed how much he cared by allowing me to breathe and see another day. I had been on the rough streets of Jackson searching for my next fix, and I couldn't thank the Lord enough for seeing me through all of that. I'd been shot, lost the love of my life, and I was still in a battle. Not going back to the streets and the heroin was tough, but I promised myself that I'd do better and continue moving forward. I had to give it my all before the journey was over.

After an hour drive, I pulled into the graveled driveway of the graveyard. As I got closer to the gate, all I could hear was the crunchy sound of the rocks underneath the tires. A white small-sized vehicle was already parked when I got there. I murdered the engine, got out, and slowly crept to the tall black fence that fenced in the entire gravesite. An African-American mother and li'l girl stood a few feet from James' burial spot. I opened the gate and slowly moved about, stepping over grass sods still taking root over freshly dug graves. I watched the girl kiss the tombstone they visited. I made it to the father of my children's resting place. I was surprised to see that he had a headstone. Inscripted were his name, birth date, and the date he passed away. The same portrait used on his obituary was on the granite stone. He posed for the picture in a crisp white t-shirt and chucked up the deuces looking cool. I bent my knees, took a seat on the ground, and sobbed.

With my face buried in my hands, I broke down. The tears poured down like raindrops during a thunderstorm. I heard footsteps behind me. The mother and the child were leaving. I never looked up. I heard the car start and go on down the highway. I stretched my body out. I started to softly speak to the stone with my face close to the cold marble as if I was whispering in James' ear. "I never got the chance to tell you some things. Now, you're gone. You'll never know how much I loved you. I saw a change in you that I never thought I'd see. When you were off drugs, you were the perfect man. I wish that I had of been more grateful for what you did. I assumed that you'd always be around. I'm missing you so much. I never imagined being in a world without you. You're in my heart." I cried out loud, "Please, come back. Let me see you one more time. I need you!"

The more I wiped my eyes, the more the water seemed to fall down and drop onto the ground. Between sobs, I was able to say, "I love you and one day we'll see each other again." I cried so long and hard that my throat hurt. It was all out of frustration because no matter what I did or attempted to do, I could never bring him back.

I stood up and dusted the dirt from my clothes. As I was going back to my ride, I scoped out a white piece of paper on the grave where the other visitors' were standing. I leaned over and saw it was a handwritten note that read, *"Daddy, I'm ready for you to come home. Me and Mommy miss you so much. I baked some chocolate chip cookies yesterday, those were your favorite. Tell God and Jesus that I said hello and to take good care of you."* The child drew a huge smiley face and a heart and signed her name at the bottom, *Love, Daija.*

A deep feeling of compassion shot through my heart. The words from that small child were touching. I got out of the gate, wiped away long streams of water from my eyes, and proceeded to the car. A dark green car flew into the driveway. I took a deep breath because it was Ms. Glenda, James' mother driving up in her Cadi. I hurried to leave by hopping in my Ford Focus. I was about to pull off when she got out of her whip with a bouquet of blue and white artificial flowers. Glenda flagged me with her hand. I let the driver's side window down. "Can I help you?" I asked with sarcasm.

"You sure can. I don't want you back up here near my son's grave. You didn't try to save my baby, and I still think you're to blame for his death," she said. She had on an orange dress that stopped above the knee, orange slippers, and a black shoulder length wig with white streaks. I swear she looked like Beetlejuice by the head and a big ass round orange pumpkin from the neck down. If I didn't know any better, I would have thought she was trying to win a Halloween contest.

I waved her off. "Glenda, you ain't talking about nothing, so move around."

"You're right. I'm not talking about *nothing*. I'm talking about how you didn't give a damn 'bout my son. You didn't even have the decency to call me and let me know he had passed. I had to hear it from mothafuckas in the streets." She dropped the flowers, placed her hand on her hip, and rolled her neck while saying it. I could not get the fact that she actually left the house wearing that ugly horsehair. I let out a loud laugh and almost choked. She really thought she was fresh to def.

"You need to stop because you sound and look crazy as hell. Gon' 'head with all that." I giggled. I refused to let her ruin my day.

She pointed her finger toward me. "You're laughing now, but I'll whoop you like I'm yo' momma. Don't play games with me," she threatened.

I took a deep breath and slowly let it out. "My mama's dead, so don't let nothing about her slip out your mouth again. You up here throwing threats around, but if you hit me you better kill me."

She huffed and puffed. Then she started jumping all around like a kangaroo. She pounded her fist into the palm of her hand. "C'mon get out the car. Show me you ain't soft as tissue, hoe!" My shoulder had begun to start feeling better, so there was no way I would let her have me in pain again. I decided to put the car in drive and slowly move along down the small dusty road that would lead me to the main highway so I could go on about my business. She was on some petty shit, and I wasn't. As I proceeded to go on, I let the window up. I suddenly heard some loud talking, looked to my left, and noticed Glenda jogging beside my ride still trying to start some shit with me. She was so big that I was shocked she could walk, and here this heifer had the nerve to be trying to run. She hit the back passenger window with her fist. "Get out so I can bust yo' head open!"

"Stop hitting my goddamn car, bitch!" I shouted.

I continued to roll on, and she kept on running. I looked up in my rearview mirror. I saw her stop, lean over, and put her hands on her knees. It looked like she was panting. She quickly stood back up and ran on down some more. I could have pulled off, but several cars were coming by. I had to come to a complete stop. The cars crept by slow as turtles. "Hurry the fuck up," I mumbled to myself.

My car shook, and that made me turn around to see what was going on. OMG, the fool had jumped on my trunk. "Oh Lawd, I'm gon' have to have my struts replaced. Get yo' mothafuckin' ass off my damn car!" I yelled. I held my mouth wide open. I couldn't believe she was stupid enough to be back there like that. She was lying there with her face pressed against the rear glass and her legs dangled. "Okay, since you ain't gonna move and want to pretend that you're throwed off, I'ma show you how sick minded bitches get down. You must not know 'bout me!" I loudly stated.

I watched the last car go by. I shifted the gear in reverse and mashed the gas then came to an abrupt stop. She tumbled down to the ground and landed on her stomach. I heard a thump and heard, "Owww!" I put the whip in drive and put the pedal to the metal. Rocks spun and popped her everywhere. She'd prob'ly be hurting later on in the day and be rubbing herself down with some type of muscle rub cream. The way she slammed against that ground, I knew she was too sore to win a wrestling match against a grasshopper.

Put On The Spot

Sparkle

As I stood outside of the hospital's door, Angelica came from around the nurses' station and approached me. "Ma'am where did his son go? The doctor is ready to speak to him concerning his dad's chest x-ray that just came back," she said.

I looked down the hallway. "He and his sister should be coming back up here in a minute." I put my pointer finger up for her to hold up. "I'll go get them. Give me a few minutes to step outside."

She smiled. "I'll let Doctor Wages know that they are headed back this way."

I walked fast down the hall and continued until I found them out front. Not only did I find the two of them, but I also noticed a very familiar person arguing with Sayveon. The two of them were all up in each other's face. They were hurling insults and threats. I raced and got in the middle of the chaos. "Ontavious, what is the problem? What are you doing here?" I wanted to know and gently pressed my hand against his chest to stop him from beefing with my baby's daddy.

He slapped my hand away. "Man, this is the kind of shit you're out here doing and making a damn fool out of me. I told you I wasn't coming to Mama V's engagement party, but something wouldn't let me miss it. I left work early to surprise you there. I'll be damned if you didn't leave with this ignorant ass dude that never did anything but play you," he snapped. From his clothing, I knew he was telling the truth. He dressed for the occasion in a pair of dark black dress slacks, a crisp black and white striped button down shirt, and a pair of charcoal-black stylish lace-up crocodile skin shoes.

Carmen tossed her cigarette down. She stood in front of Sayveon to keep him from getting at Ontavious. Those two fools were out there going ham. I looked directly into Ontavious' eyes, and I could see the hurt that I had caused him. I knew he was the best choice for me, but I didn't want to cause him any pain. "Baby, I only came up here to comfort him because his dad crashed the party and ended up having to be picked up by an ambulance. I wasn't doing nothing but being a friend," I explained. I cocked my head to the side wondering how in the hell he knew I was up there in the first place. "How'd you find out that I was here?" I asked.

"Don't worry about all of that," he said.

I had gotten nervous. Butterflies swarmed through my stomach from the anxiety and stress of seeing my boyfriend. I had to come up with something to calm the situation down. Sayveon stood a few feet from us going off. "Nigga you ain't gangsta. You pussy," he insulted.

Ontavious faced Sayveon. "Don't let this pretty boy look fool you. You better know what you're doing when you run up on this." I had never heard him talk like that before. It was so out of character for him, but I think everyone has a li'l hood in them when provoked because what happened next had me trippin'.

Sayveon balled his fists, rushed Ontavious, and hit him in the face. Ontavious threw a punch right back that slammed against Sayveon's eye. I knew that situation had gone too far, and now they were duking it out. Before I knew it, they were on the ground going ape. They rolled all around on the grass punching each other. Sayveon found a way to get from underneath and began hammering Ontavious. Bam! Bam! Bam! Ontavious was trying to block the hits, but he was still getting nailed. I'm riveted, glued to the scene thinking, "Are these two fools really going stupid like this?"

"Stop it!" I yelled and pushed Sayveon, who didn't budge an inch. A big dark skinned security guard stormed out, pulled him off Ontavious, and let him go. Ontavious hopped to his feet, tackled Sayveon down and started throwing hands like they were sledgehammers.

Carmen stepped over and started punching Ontavious in the back of the head yelling, "Get off my fucking brother!"

"Hoe ass trick, don't touch my goddamn man!" I screamed. I kicked her in the side. I loved kicking mothafuckas so I had some good footwork. I took her down and clocked her in the face a few times. Big dude grabbed me and tossed me to the side. I was a lightweight midget compared to that giant.

"You ain't gotta be throwing me and shit," I lashed out at the guard. My ass was chilly and that's when I detected that my dress was up to my stomach. While I was putting that work on ole' girl, it had to have crept up. I snatched the end of the dress back down, panting and trying to catch my breath.

"Get the fuck off the property and go home!" big guy ordered, breathing hard. His forehead had plenty of frowns. Nobody moved; we just stood there looking. "Now! Can y'all fucking hear?!!"

Sayveon and Ontavious both took their shirts off and tossed them on the ground. They squared off and threw more punches. It lasted for a couple of minutes going back and forth. They were clocking each other with shots to the face and body, but nothing with knock out power. Then it happened, Sayveon got in a solid shot to Ontavious' jaw and dropped him. Ontavious crumbled to the ground. Sayveon started gloating. "I'm a G from the streets." He talked big.

"Aren't you gonna do something?" I asked the guard who just stood there.

"Hell, nah. If they want to keep going at it, then I ain't gon' stop it again," he shot back and watched.

Ontavious shook his head, got up, cleared the fog, and wanted some more.

"Aight. C'mon. I'm 'bout to murder this clown," Sayveon boasted. He rushed at him and right before he swung off, his eyes got big and he paused. I couldn't figure out what the hell had just happened to make him stop in his tracks like that. "That's how you wanna do it? Let me get to my whip, and I got you." I didn't understand the reason for him telling him that. He broke toward the parking garage, but it was too late. Ontavious had charged his way and stabbed him with a pocketknife dead on the right side of his butt cheek. Sayveon jumped around in a circle hollering, "This mothafucka done shanked me in the ass!"

Ontavious took off running and left Sayveon bunny hopping around hollering, cussing, and fussing. The guard laughed so hard he choked on his own spit. Damn, I never expected that shit to happen.

It Ain't Over Yet

Sayveon

The weak ass mothafucka that was claiming Sparkle had punctured my ass. I mean literally. Only a coward mofo would do that kind of shit. Here I was lying in the same hospital that my old man was in. The only difference between him and I was he had some major concerns going on. I didn't know if he'd make it through. I lay on my side in the Emergency Room, contemplating my next move. Sparkle stood beside the bed comforting me by rubbing her fingers through my dreads and singing my favorite gospel tune, 'His Eye Is On The Sparrow.' She knew me well, and over the years, she would sing that song to me when I felt down and out.

I leaned my head back and enjoyed the sound of her voice. Sparkle could blow, but she always turned down singing in front of large crowds. She was shy when it came to showing off her God given talent. The way she cared for me in that small room that night, I had no doubt in my mind that I'd be trying to re-wife her. I was shown right then that she was the one, and I was salty that I hadn't appreciated her in the past. She was always there when I needed her and that meant a lot to a street hustler like me because I trusted few and had to watch many. Whenever I needed a lift, she was there to help me stand and get back right. I didn't realize how much I loved and needed her until she walked out on me.

I closed my eyes and pictured us walking down the aisle together and having a nice sized family. Fuck being alone and a bachelor in a big house, having to sleep by myself every night. I wanted a woman who I could trust to be there no matter what. I squenched my eyes tighter when the searing burn flared up, consuming me in agony and making my mind go blank. As I laid there, I couldn't help but say to myself that I was getting back all of my dirt and wrongs. Shit like this wasn't supposed to happen to me; I was too gangsta. I chalked it up though and accepted it as bad karma. It was only a matter of time before a nigga touched me, but I'd make sure he got touched back.

Leaving The Past Alone

Stephanie

Dealing with Glenda had me upset. It was a sin and a shame that she had to be handled like that. I pushed on down the highway and decided to go to Aunt Ruby's house to see what she was up to. Auntie always had the best advice and knew exactly what to say to make me feel better. She was also a good listener and could keep me laughing. The ride to her place was exactly what I needed to ease my mind. I turned the music off and enjoyed the peace and quiet. Riding through the countryside, I had the chance to see the pleasant blue sky, green grass, wooden fences with farm animals inside walking around, and feel the wind brushing past, rustling the trees and causing the leaves to tumble to the rich soil.

The clouds had turned grey, and the sun went into hiding. Raindrops began to tumble down on my windshield and sounded like pattering footsteps. A few minutes had gone by when I rolled into Auntie Ruby's driveway. When I pulled up, I noticed her sitting on the porch with her head down. She had on a white house gown with black house shoes and a black bonnet covering her hair. She quickly glanced up and dropped her head back down.

"Hey there, lady," I addressed her and had a seat in a rocker.

"Hey, babydoll," she spoke back in a low voice.

"What's the matter?" I could tell that something was bothering her, bad.

"I ain't seen Harry in a while. I reckon something came through and killed him. These coyotes are bad at night. They'll attack chickens, hens, and roosters in a minute. I'll have to get another one, or I may just decide not to. I'm not sure." She gave me a half-smile. "What brings you this way?" She switched topics.

"I went to James' grave, and his momma ended up driving up there when I was leaving. I'm tired of that woman accusing me of having something to do with the death of her son. She first said that she thought I had done something to kill him. Now she's accusing me of some more mess. I can't deal," I vented. I chuckled before saying, "She even jumped on top of my trunk when I was leaving, and she's as big as a barrel."

Auntie snickered. "You better than me because I would have got out of my car and beat her ass until she couldn't stand up straight." She got silent and cleared her throat before dropping some knowledge on me. "After a death, people go through four stages. That's shock, denial, pain, and then reality. It's shocking when a tragedy happens when the person isn't expected to pass away so soon. Then they're in denial and trying to find someone to blame for the death because it seems so unreal. After that, the hurt and pain comes down because they've loss someone who meant so much. Next, reality comes, and they eventually deal with the death and the realness that the person will never come back again. Allow her to go through those four things, and don't have nothing to do with her until she gets over it. Right now that woman is angry that her child is gone, and you're the only one for her to point the finger at."

What she said made so much sense. "You're so right." I crossed my leg, leaned back in the rocking chair, and rocked back and forth.

"After my husband passed away, it was almost too much to bear. I didn't want to go on living without him. In time the shock wore off and reality set in. To say that I'm completely over it now would be an unrealistic thing to admit. Being honest, I still go in and out, up and down, in a journey of acceptance and denial, missing and yearning, believing and disbelieving. Closure and acceptance are myths, not milestones. After all of these years, I can't say that I feel better. No. I feel different, and I can breathe now. You don't get over it, under it, or around it. You get through it. It kills you, and yet you're still alive."

"That's all true. I think about James and I get sad, but I know I have to go on. My life can't stop here. He wouldn't listen to me telling him to stop doing the drugs, so the very things that he couldn't let go of killed him." During our discussion, a fly kept flying in my face. I waved my hand back and forth, and he eventually went away then came right back. She reached over, picked up the flyswatter, and popped me right on the head. I jumped and wondered what the hell she had done that for.

"That li'l nasty bastard landed on your hair," she told me. The dead insect dropped to the concrete.

"James should have left that dope alone. You couldn't stop him from doing that. That's a decision he would have had to make." She started back talking like ain't nothing happened. Dang, country folks just didn't give a damn.

"I still hurt though, and I miss him."

She grabbed my hand and held on to it. "Focus on the gifts and blessings of having him in your life. Think about the miracles of his life rather than the tragedy of his death. Some days you'll do better than others. That's the nature of grief. The roller coaster ride is not as painful as it was in the beginning. Like my missing him, it is never likely to end." She let go of my hand and continued on, "Focus on opening your heart and living rather than searching for closure and acceptance. Fighting on and living each day to its fullest, opening our hearts to those we love and being brave just may be the best and highest expressions of our lasting love."

I stood and hugged her. "You got a way of making me feel better, Auntie."

"I've already been where you're trying to go. Now, sit your fast butt down and tell me about what happened with you in that man's bedroom." She was ready for me to spill the tea and gossip, which was what she lived for.

I giggled a bit. "His wife caught me sleeping in the bed with her husband, and I ended up getting shot. That woman was a lunatic and…"

She interrupted before I could finish. "Were you butt ass naked?" she inquired, being nosy and not cracking a smile.

I fell out laughing. "No Auntie. I had my clothes on. I was lying down; nothing went on that night."

"You sho' he wasn't over there thumping yo' thighs?"

"Nah. None of that went down." My aunt wasn't nothing but an old freak.

"Well, let me ask it another way. Did he hide the snake in the bush?"

"Auntie, no." Lawd the woman was hornier than a dog in heat.

"Well, I'm glad you're okay. Messing with somebody else's man can get you in a lot of trouble. That was a lesson learned, and don't make that same mistake again," she preached.

"I will do better." I had been so wrapped up in our conversation that I forgot to ask where my sister was. Her vehicle wasn't in the yard. "Where's Sparkle and the baby?"

"She left about ten minutes before you pulled up. She took the baby shopping with her to go and try to find her something to wear tonight. She's supposed to be going to an engagement party somewhere in Jackson."

We continued talking and laughing. She gave me some good words of wisdom that day. I loved speaking with her because she was encouraging and hilarious all at the same time. We went on and on for a few hours. Seeing Auntie was exactly what I needed to clear my head of Glenda and all of the other crazy shit I had going on in my life.

***

That night I had been invited to the 39th birthday celebration for one of my first cousins, Deuce. I looked like a chicken with its head cut off running around the apartment getting dressed to go out. After showering, I took off to the closet with a towel wrapped around me to find an outfit that I could be comfortable in and feel confident. I chose my fit and lotioned my body down. I grabbed my gear and got dressed in a black low-neck mini- dress. I slipped my feet into my black leather knee high six-inch stiletto boots with a pink bottom. I applied my make-up, and brushed my hair down which was styled in a shoulder length wrap. I checked myself out in the mirror to make sure I was looking good enough to eat, and yes, I was. Shit, I'd have niggas tryna put me on a plate and sop me up with a biscuit.

Once I got in the car, I hit Sparkle up on her cell. She answered on the first ring. "Hello."

"What it do, girl?" I asked, in a cheery tone.

"At the hospital with Sayveon, girl. How 'bout Ontavious stabbed him in the ass?"

"What the fuck?!! Girl, please tell me you lying!" I burst out laughing so hard I damn near ran off the road and almost pissed on myself in the process. "Good. He has finally met his match."

"Well, they were going head up at first, and both of them were swinging blows. Sayveon had gotten the best of Ontavious, and that's when he pulled out a pocket knife. The doctor's say he'll be okay, but he lost a lot of blood. They're going to give him a tetanus shot and a few stitches. They'll keep him overnight just to observe him."

"Good. Well, are you staying all night or what?"

"He told me to get his car and go home to be with Layla and come back tomorrow morning and stay with him. I'm almost to his car now. Pops is in the same hospital because he wanted to show his ass and decided to come in and crash Mama V's party. He and her cousins were fighting and everything. It was just messy. He dropped to the floor, and the paramedics came and got him. Something is blocking his bowels, and Carmen came to the door a few minutes ago and said that he has pneumonia too."

"Goddamn. Payback is kicking their asses, huh?"

"Guess so."

I cleared my throat. "How did Ontavious end up around Sayveon anyway?"

"He first told me he wasn't going to Mama V's party because he had to work late, but he changed his mind and showed up. Well, I had already left with

Sayveon going to the hospital where Pops was. He saw my car still there and asked where I was. Somebody there must've told him that I left with Sayveon and we went to Mississippi Baptist Hospital."

"Umph...Umph...Umph." I shook my head because the shit was a disaster. "To clear your mind, you should come kick back with me tonight," I offered, hoping she'd accept.

"Where are you headed?"

"To Deuce's birthday party," I revealed.

"Sounds like fun. I'll come and hang out for a li'l bit. I'm already dressed for something like that."

I gave her the address, and we agreed to hang out for a while. I hated to see baby-sister going through all of the unnecessary bull. Hopefully she would be able to keep her mind off of the stuff that went on that day with her, and I'd be relieved of the stress I went through earlier in my day as well. I wanted us to party like some rockstars.

Splashing Out

Sparkle

The parking lot of the three- story club Dreamz located on the corner of Gallatin and West Capitol streets had a lot full of luxury whips. I drove up and found a space in between two new-modeled vehicles, a silver Audi A7 and a black Mercedes Benz S-Class. I let down the mirror clipped to the sun visor and fixed my hair and applied a fresh coat of lip-gloss and popped my lips. Once I got out, I sashayed pass a few dudes who were posted up against their cars shooting the breeze with one another. I could hear the loud rap music booming from inside.

Stephanie was outside of the club shivering in the cold, waiting for me. When she saw me, all I saw was her perfect smile, and we embraced. The huge door attendant asked us both for our ID and checked them out, took the cover charge, and wished us a fun night. We stepped on in, and there had to be at least twenty-five plasma TV screens, VIP rooms, three bars, and three dance floors. The place was cluttered with broads and niggas everywhere. Stephanie and I stood against the wall until we spotted our cousin mingling and shaking hands with lots of people. We made our way over to him. When he spotted us, his eyes lit up.

"My mothafuckin' cousins are in the house!" Deuce hollered over the music. He was geared down in all Polo. It was his night, and he shined as bright as the iced-out diamond chain around his neck.

Everyone knew that Deuce was a dopeboy and had that major paper. He was well known in the Jackson area, and he had the reputation of taking no shit from nobody. He was laid-back and had a giving heart, but he could turn into a killer in a matter of seconds. He had gone to prison a while back and served a ten-year bid for drug-trafficking, but when he touched down, he came back even harder and was right back slanging that work. Nevertheless, he was getting that paper, so I respected his hustle.

Deuce took us up to the VIP area and told us to grab a seat at an empty table. He told one of his boys to go get us some bottles of liquor.

We were in swag central. The ballers in that section held bottles in one hand and racks in the other. There were a few thirsty tricks dancing and prancing all around hoping this was their come-up. Ciroc, Henny, Grey Goose, Dom Perignon, and Remy were poured up by the splurgers. I overheard one of the big timers saying he was about to pour some lean. He stepped over to one of the tables, tipped over one of the pint sized bottles, and sipped it through a straw from his plastic cup. A few men stood bouncing to the music looking stupid fresh in their thugged out fits, smoking swishers and 'dranking' that 'act right.' Touch screen camera phones and Iphones took pictures of the scenery, and they posed, flossing.

My cousin's people came back and put two bottles in front of us, Goose and New Amsterdam. He also had two cups of ice and placed them down. "If y'all need anything else, get at me," he said to us, then turned and walked off. I twisted the top off the Goose and poured me and Steph a cup, and we sipped and bobbed our heads to the music. When the rap had gone off, a slower tune by Mary J. Blige played, 'Mr. Wrong.' So many women's hands rose in the air and slowly moved from side to side.

"That's my shit," one of the pigeons at a spot directly in front of us said aloud. The female stood in front of the dude seated with his boys all around him. From watching him, I knew he was a Boss. He tossed money around and paid for everybody's drinks. He had a certain arrogance, but it wasn't aggravating. Actually, it turned me on. I loved a man that had a bit of cockiness and confidence. The gold diggers peeped his style too because they were all over him like stink on shit.

The rat had on a silver and black open back super-short dress with a pair of silvery suede open toe high-heeled pumps. She bent all the way over in the Boss' face, moving her ass from side to side. Her almost closed eyes told me that she was under the influence. She had to be either high or drunk. Her black thong showed, and I almost fell out of the chair when I saw something hanging out of it. WTF!

"Bitch, I kno' you ain't on yo' rag and over here trying to sweat a nigga's dick," dude said in a loud voice to her. The long white string dangled down the whole time she popped her ass. She was on something that had her in a zone because I don't think she heard him. She kept right on dancing and even made her boodie clap. The people surrounding her laughed and pointed at the tampon string hanging from her coodie hole.

Steph leaned over to my ear. "Now, that hoe needs a good ass whooping for that shit right there."

I giggled and continued sipping on my drink.

The big baller raised his foot and kicked her in the butt, hard. The young woman stumbled forward and grabbed a hold of a chair for support. She clung there, mouth-hanging open and slumped over for a long time before she begged, "Somebody help me up." A youngster beside her helped her over to the corner of a wall and sat her down. Her head leaned over. She eventually laid down on the floor, and the partying continued.

The person who kicked the girl in the butt turned around, and Stephanie caught his attention. He gave her a wide smile, stood, and stepped over to where we were seated. "What it do, sexy?" he asked her.

"Hello," she spoke back.

"Is anyone sitting here?" he asked, referring to an empty chair beside her.

"Nope."

"I'm Tank and you are?" he questioned her after introducing himself.

"I'm Stephanie, and this is my sister, Sparkle."

They chatted back and forth, and then he called for someone who had just come up to the area rolling six deep with his crew. "Ay, Buck!"

Buck twisted around and came over. "What's the deal, my nigga?" he directed at Tank, and the two dapped fists.

"I want you to meet Sparkle, and Sparkle this is my homeboy, Buck," Tank introduced us and started back spitting in my sister's ear.

"How you doing Miss Lady?" he wanted to know and sat down in an empty seat beside me. The six goons with him found chairs at our table. A few brought seats from another empty table and made themselves comfortable. They sipped and got tipsy off the drinks in their hands while I conversed with the muscle of their team.

"You drinking good, or you wanna hit some of this?" he asked.

"I'm straight. This liquor got me feeling damn good right about now." I looked over at him, checking him out. He was ruggedly handsome, not pretty boy attractive. He had long dreads with cinnamon-brown tips and built with a smooth dark-chocolate complexion. He took off his leather jacket, and I noticed that he was tatted up. He pulled a pocket full of dead faces out and told a youngster from his click, "Go cop me some more liquor and bring nothing but the best brands back." He had a half-empty pint of Bacardi. He hit it straight to the neck from the bottle, no cup. Buck was thuggin' it out.

Buck's boy came back with five bottles. Cristal, Courvoisier, and Patron were in one hand, and Bacardi and Moet hung from the other. He gave them all to Buck who made sure his boys were drinking good and made sure they all had some alcohol. He handed me the Patron. "I see you got your own shit, but that right there is on me, babygirl."

"Thank you," I said.

We held an interesting conversation for the next fifteen minutes or so. A slow song came on during our chat. Stephanie and her new friend stood, along with other couples in that section, and slow danced to the music.

"I'm gonna take y'all back to the 90's with this one. This is Honey Love by your boy R. Kelly," the DJ announced into the microphone.

Buck grabbed my hand. I stood to my feet. He held his hands against my hips while I draped my arms on his shoulders. We then moved to the music. Our bodies were close, and we hugged and swayed to the sounds of the melody.

"You're beautiful," he complimented in my ear.

I blushed. "Do you say that to all the young ladies you meet?"

"Nah. I don't be sweatin' these thirsty tricks out here like that, shawdy." He looked right into my eyes. "If you weren't looking all fly and shit, you wouldn't have me dropping lines on you."

I let out a cute giggle. He got even closer, and the seat of his crotch centered between my thighs. His rock hardness had gotten my panties wet. The smell of his cologne had me super moist. When the song went off, we moved back to our places and had a seat until the sound of booty shaking music hit the airway. I hopped up and bounced my ass up against him. He matched my rhythm. Stephanie and her friend got up too. We all danced to the sounds of the beat. I normally didn't act so wild, but that night I didn't care. Ratchet on deck. Fuck it. We only live once, so I danced the night away without a care in the world.

A Rough Morning

Sparkle

The sound of my daughter's crying woke me out of my sleep. I could hear Aunt Ruby walking through the house telling her to calm down. I figured Layla must have been hungry, and my aunt gave her a bottle. That's when I noticed how dry my mouth was, and I was thirsty. My head hurt, and the strong taste of alcohol lingered on my tongue. My eyes felt tight, and the sunlight beaming through the window nearly blinded me. I rubbed my stomach because it burned inside. I tried to lift my head but quickly dropped it back down to the pillow. The pounding headache made it hard to think because it felt like my brain had been removed and replaced with cotton balls and needles. Goddamn, I was fucked up.

Aunt Ruby knocked on my door. That's when I noticed that I couldn't take any noise louder than a whisper.

"Huh?" I said in a groggy and grumpy kind of way.

She opened the door and peeped her head in. "I hate to bother you, but Ontavious is in the living room. He says he needs to see you."

I waved her off. "I ain't trying to hear nothing that nigga is talking about. Tell him to go home," I rudely ordered and turned from my back to my side. The whole room looked mighty funny, and the next thing I knew, I was leaned over throwing up in the garbage can beside the bed. Auntie ran out of the room and came back holding a small white towel in her hand. She gave it to me and told me to wash my face off and clean myself up. I wiped my lips and placed my head on the pillow. That's when more puke shot from my stomach. I tried to get to the wastebasket but instead vomit landed all over the floor.

"Girl, you musta got drunk last night? This room smells like a liquor factory. That shit is coming out of your pores." She leaned over while holding Layla and sniffed. "Good God. You got this whole room smelling like vomit and booze."

"I'm sorry. I got a hangover, and I'm not in the mood to talk to anybody," I grumbled. My aunt worked my last nerve and didn't make the headache I had feel any better. I wished that she and Ontavious would leave me alone. I didn't feel like being bothered.

"Sorry ain't gonna get it. Get up out of this bed and see about this baby. I'm going to church this morning." She placed Layla on the bed. Layla made cooing noises and was ready to play. She grabbed a handful of my hair and put it in her mouth.

I raised up to stop her and nearly collapsed. I couldn't move. My head throbbed. I could've sworn somebody was beating drums inside of it. I rubbed my forehead and sighed. I got the baby's hands and finally pried her fingers from my hair. She hollered.

"Look li'l girl. It is not time for this. Momma is not feeling good, and you are all up in my ear." The screaming made me cringe. She was upset that I wouldn't let her have her way.

Aunt Ruby was about to go out of the door. She twisted around toward me and placed her hand on her hip. "I'm gonna do you the same way my mother did me on a Sunday morning after I partied all Saturday night and got boozed up."

"What's that?" I moaned.

"You need to get dressed and get the baby ready. Y'all are going to church with me. Now, get ya butt up and c'mon because you're driving."

I rolled over on my stomach and gagged into the wastebasket, coughing and spitting. "I can't make it. I'll go next Sunday," I tried to bargain.

"Hell no. I said get up, and that's what I mean. If you can go out and serve the devil, you surely can rise up this morning and serve the good Lawd," she lectured. Aunt Ruby walked out and closed the door behind her. I reached over and grabbed my cell phone resting underneath the other pillow. I checked my call log and saw that Sayveon had called me four times. Then, I saw a text message that he sent, Call me when you get up. A nurse told me that I should be being discharged after twelve o'clock.

"Oh, shit," I said in a low tone. I dialed his number, and he answered on the first ring. "Hey, what's up?" I could hardly get the words out because I was so fucked up and sick.

"Dayum, you sound bad. You just waking up? I been blowing you up all morning."

"I'm up; I was about to get dressed to go to church. Do you want me to come on and get you?"

"Nah. Go on to church, and I'll text you when I get to the crib. I have someone else who can come get me." He got silent for a minute when he heard Layla giggling. She made noise while she played with her toes, putting them in her mouth. I let her do her thing and slowly got up and went over to the closet and got out outfits for me and her. Sayveon and I ended the call. I slowly maneuvered my way back to the bed and washed her up. I changed her diaper and put a purple dress with matching leggings on her. I put her shoes on and then combed her hair. She was set and looking cute. I snatched my head back fast when I heard two knocks.

"Yes, Auntie," I dryly said. I was 'bout tired of her for the morning, making me get up and dragging me to church. I had gotten throwed and could barely hold my head up.

The door opened and Ontavious stood there staring at me. "Who in the hell gave you permission to come up in here?" I snapped.

"Your aunt told me that it was okay."

"Well, it's not." I sat down in a chair that was close to the bedroom door with my daughter in my arms. I waited to see how this shit would turn out.

"We need to talk."

I dropped my head and rubbed the back of my neck. "Right now, I don't feel like talking to you or anybody else. The way you acted last night really upset me because I went to the hospital to make sure that Pops was okay; it wasn't like you caught me somewhere having sex."

He held his hand up. "There's no need to explain. I'm not even mad." He held his hand out. "Give me my ring back because it's over between us."

My heart dropped. I mean, I knew I was in the wrong for even going to the hospital with Sayveon when I had a man, but I did it out of concern. Guess he didn't see it that way. I pulled the ring from my finger and tossed it to the floor. He reached over, retrieved it, and faced me. "I left every woman that I was associating with alone to make it work between me and you. I wanted to be a good man, and I thought I had found the woman who would appreciate me and love me forever. I was wrong. You're no better than any other female that's walking around here playing niggas and living double lives. Well, a young woman that I was dealing with before you is ready to be the woman that I need. I've decided to end things with you for good and move on." He dropped a ton of bricks on me with that speech.

I put Layla in her playpen and slapped the cowboy shit out of him. "Mothafucka, you got huge balls to step off on my turf telling me that you got a new trick," I snapped off. "Get the fuck up out of my face, and if I never see you again, that'll be a blessing."

He walked away without uttering one word. I never expected him to say those words to me. My heart had been snatched out. I was more than hurt. I was devastated and felt shitted on, but I was so used to dealing with a dirty nigga that although the situation was painful, I knew I'd get over it. Time heals all wounds. This wound would ache for a while, but one day it will be alright and there will no longer be a sore but only a scar left to remind me that pain doesn't last always. I'd be okay in due time. Until that day came, I'd have to endure it all. I should have known that he was too good to be true. He wasn't shit.

Praising The Lord

Sparkle

Auntie and I walked into the small country church and walked down the aisle. Women had on huge brimmed hats and nice dresses. The men wore crisp white shirts and ties with their suits. Most of the li'l girls had nice neat ponytails, stockings and dresses and dressy shoes. The boys had fresh haircuts and dressed in their best too. We found a seat on the fifth pew. Sunday morning worship service started. The pianist played, and the choir director directed the choir members to stand in their yellow and gold robes. They sang a spiritual tune. Aunt Ruby moved from side to side enjoying the sound of the music. The back door opened, and I took a quick glance behind me. Ontavious held the door open for a chick that came in the building. She was brown-skinned, thick, and slightly shorter than me.

"I know he didn't bring that hussy up in here," I softly spoke into Aunt Ruby's ear.

"Who is that?" she asked looking puzzled.

"I'll tell you about it when we get home."

When the choir finished singing three different hymns, the preacher got up from behind the pulpit and took the microphone. He started his sermon. The only thing I remembered after that was being nudged. "Wake your butt up," Auntie fussed. Layla was asleep in her arms. I wiped the corner of my mouth, yawned, and sat up straight. I had drifted off to sleep.

I looked around and saw Ontavious with his arms around the female he said was his woman now. I woke up hoping that this was all a dream.

Pastor Jamison Wilson finished preaching, and it was time for people to stand up and testify. A little thin elderly woman with white hair rose up from her seat. "Giving all glory to God who is the head of my life. To the Pastor and First Lady, all the elders of the church, and to all my saints and friends. I want to thank the Lord for all that he has done and is doing for me. When I look back over my life, I can truly say that I've been blessed."

She burst out yelling and jumped up and down with her cane in her hand. "Y'all don't hear me in here today!" She caught the Holy Ghost and tap danced before catching her breath and calming down a bit. "My soul cries out, Hallelujah!" She stopped and held her hand up high. "The devil has been trying to mess with me, but my God has me covered and knocked him down. Y'all keep me in your prayers, and I'll keep y'all in mine too."

"Amen," the worshippers said.

She sat, and the next old man in his late sixties stood. "I just want to thank the man above who looks high but sees down low. I have a neighbor who moved in right next door to me about a year ago. He got mad with me because he said I'm too spiritual. So, after a month of me yelling, 'Praise the Lord', from my porch he would go outside on his porch and yell, 'There is no Lord'."

He smiled and then continued. "The other day when it was storming and raining, I couldn't go to the store for food because of the weather. I barely had anything in my house to eat. I went outside, raised my hands to the sky, and said, 'Lord I can't get to the store to get grocery. It's storming and lightening and I don't have no mo' food.' The next morning I went outside and there were bags of food on the porch, enough to last a week. 'Praise the Lord' I yelled. My neighbor stepped out of his house and said, 'There is no God. I bought those groceries.' My neighbor started laughing and making fun of me. I raised my hands up and said, 'Praise the Lord. You sent me groceries and made the devil pay for them'."

Lots of laughter filled the room after his testimony. Service soon ended. On the way out, everyone greeted one another and gave handshakes and hugs with big smiles. "Nice to see you again, sister," the preacher said as I was going out.

"I enjoyed service." I looked around and noticed Ontavious coming out behind me. Aunt Ruby had Layla and was speaking to the members and holding conversations with a few of them.

I got to the Beamer and got inside. I was cool with seeing Ontavious and the new woman in his life at first, but suddenly I got heated and got out and strutted over to his ride. He held the truck door open for the stank hoe while she got in.

"Excuse me, but you ain't nothing. How you gonna bring this woman to church? We ain't been broke up long, and this is the kind of mess that you're pulling on me?" I wanted to know. I was furious.

"Who is she, baby?" the woman asked.

"Nobody," he had the nerve to say.

"Nobody? Oh, now you acting brand new on me like you don't kno' who the hell I am?" I went off, snapping. Before I knew it, I gave him a hard push.

"Keep your hands off of me. I ain't touching you so I don't need you pushing on me. You're making yourself look stupid." He moved around me and walked over to the driver's side of his whip, slid behind the steering wheel, started the engine and drove off leaving me standing there.

A few of the church's members who stood outside conversing turned and looked in our direction. My loud voice and the tone I used had caused a scene. I was so shame that I went on about my business and got back in Sayveon's ride. I didn't think I would act a fool, but I never realized how much I cared about Ontavious until I saw him with another. That was enough to break my heart.

Disloyalty Shows Up

Sayveon

Ginger looked fucked up when she came to pick me up from the hospital that afternoon. She came up to the bed where I sat on the side of it. She had come alone. Jia hit me up earlier on my cellie and told me that she was bailing out to head back to Florida. Ginger had a busted face and hopped around on a crutch. I had smashed her shit in the other day when I went in on her.

Snowbunny had a fat busted lip and a big black circle around her eye. I gave her the ass whoopin' she needed and checked her good. Hoes out here had to be dealt wit' like that. I couldn't play handle the broad.

"Hi, Daddy," she said hopping over to me.

"What's good?"

She didn't reply but looked at me. "Are you ready?"

I got up and a nurse came in and helped me into a wheelchair. Pillows had been placed in it to help ease the pain from the stab wound I had. It took a few minutes before I could stand up.

"Hold my hand, Mr. Travis," the nurse said and put her hands around my waist to help me out.

"Nah. I'm good. I'll do it on my own." I took my time.

The nurse wheeled me into the hallway, and a CNA came and took me to the front lobby. Ginger had her car parked not far from door. I got in her ride, and we soon peeled off. During the ride to my crib, I looked over at Ginger and kind of felt bad for the way I had pounded her out and busted up her face and shit.

She glimpsed over while wheeling her car. Then she made a painful moaning noise. She slowed for a red light ahead. I was glad her good leg wasn't fucked up and she could at least get me to the crib.

"Sayveon. We need to discuss some serious business that cannot wait another minute," she told me. I could sense that this conversation would be on the serious tip.

"What's up?"

"I've had time to think a lot of things over. You are disrespectful, and you haven't been treating me as if I'm your girlfriend. You put your child's mother over me several times. I've had enough of it and you too."

"Tell me what you're saying. Stop wasting time and go ahead and give me the real."

"I'm no longer going to be with you. It's officially over between us and I'm not going to do your drug runs for you any longer."

"Fuck you mean?"

"I am saying that I will not work for you anymore and after today I won't ever contact you again." Her blue eyes stared right back before she redirected her attention back to the street.

"Bitch, you ain't goin' nowhere. If it weren't for me you wouldn't be making all the paper that you getting from the streets. You can't up and tell me that you bouncing out and think that everythang is good." I bitch slapped her.

She flinched and put her hand up to her jaw. "I'm tired of the way that you treat me. I'm starting my own operation and I have people lined up already who are willing to help me."

The feeling of betrayal and anger boiled my insides and had me fired up.

"The only way you can get out of working for me is if you die. I don't trust you hoe. You kno' too much of my business. I've trusted you and let you in my circle and now you backstabbing me. Let me find out you on some bullshit," I threatened.

"Really, Sayveon? You're making threats now?" She bust a left and cruised down my street. "I've been loyal, and I've been good to you, but I'm ready to be on my own and do my own thing. You can't get mad because I'm trying to go solo." She made an effort to explain, but I wasn't hearing it.

"You bet not get out of line. You better slow down and not get ahead of yourself. I ain't letting you go nowhere, and that's just what it is."

"You don't have to give me permission. I've spoken and told you what I am going to do, so I'm finished talking about it." She pulled up at the front of my crib and parked.

"If you go ahead and grab your own soldiers and start making paper out here, I'ma kno' that you don't like living. Bitch ass hoe, I'll murder yo' punk ass. Think it's a joke, and you'll be on yo' back wit' yo' eyelids shut tight."

Ginger turned and faced me. "Sayveon, I've had enough of your shit. You're not the big bad wolf, and I'm not one of the scary three little pigs."

I rubbed the back of my neck and got out of her car. I made a mental note to get at Ginger another time on some real shit. The only thang on my mind was getting my body back right so that I could set some thangs straight out here. These monkey ass fools were starting to not take me seriously. In due time, I'd have to pull some cards and show 'em that I'm 'bout that life. I ain't the average nigga out here.

Once I made it in my pad, I got wit' Carmen to check on Pops. She picked up on the second ring.

"What's up, Sayveon?" she said into the receiver.

"What's poppin' off babygirl?"

"Everything is fine around here as of now. Dad is doing well after his surgery this morning. The doctor performed an Intestinal obstruction repair, which is the surgery to relieve the bowel obstruction. The anesthesia is slowly wearing off. He's also on an antibiotic to clear the pneumonia. I think he's going to make a full recovery. I've decided to wait until he's better before I go back to Florida." She sneezed twice.

"Bless you," I said.

"Thank you. It's so cold in this place. I am probably coming down with a cold. Anyway, are you feeling any better?"

"I'm gon' be aight. I'm kickin' back and laying low til' I bounce back. Soon as I heal up, I'll be checking up on the old man."

"Good. I'll let him know that you called and asked about him."

"Aight. I'll holla back."

"Before you go I have something to say to you."

"I'm listening."

"I'm not trying to get in your business, but you should probably leave your child's mother alone. You two aren't good for each other. I mean, you could have gotten killed by that guy that came up here acting stupid the other night. I'm only looking out for you and your best interest."

"I appreciate it. It's all on me that you got caught up in the mix of all that bullshit, but I got this right here. Me and Sparkle cool, and I ain't got my ass on all of that right now. I'm focusing on healing so I can get back on top of my business."

"Okay. I'll let you go now and good luck."

"Later."

I hung up and took a short nap on the sofa. I had drifted off into a deep sleep until I heard a lot of commotion at the doorstep. At first, I thought I was still dreaming until I heard more hard knocks. I hopped up, went to the door, and peeped out of the peephole. A tall Caucasian dude around 6'3 with a bald head and olive skin tone stood there. I didn't kno' who he was or why he was there. He held a black briefcase in his hand and a large plastic container with dollars inside. He had on a white shirt and black slacks.

"Who is it?" I asked.

"Hi. If you don't mind I would like to talk to you about the Mississippi Children's Foundation. Would you be so kind as to let me speak with you? Or, if you are too busy, I would appreciate it if you would be generous enough to donate to a worthy cause."

"I might give you some money. Hol' up."

After all of the wrong I had been doing and the payback that was biting me in the ass, I decided to support. I felt that it would be my good deed for the day and maybe God would let up on me.

I reached in my pocket, peeled off a c-note, and opened the door.

"I hate to disturb you, but this is to help underprivileged children in certain parts of the state who are hungry and going without food," he went on to tell me.

"I understand." I handed him the one hundred dollar bill. "There you go. Have a good day."

The man gave me a huge grin. "Thank you so kindly. You are going to make a child very happy with that offering."

"Cool. Take care."

I half-way closed the door when I felt a hard push and was bum-rushed to the floor. Two more of his accomplices who I didn't even see before came in along with him with guns pointed at my head. Two white chicks with blonde hair had the barrel of their glocks aimed and ready to pull the trigger.

"What's this about? Man, I don't even kno' y'all mothafuckas," I said and wondered who sent them.

"Where is your money?" dude wanted to know.

"I got some in my pocket, and that's it. I don't keep money in my crib," I lied. I had some stashed but I wasn't about to go grab it and give it to them.

"Get down on the floor, now!" he ordered.

I dropped to my knees.

"Lay down on the fucking floor before you get your brains blown out," he warned.

I stretched out and didn't exchange words. He ran his hand down in my pocket and pulled out the three hundred dollars I had on me. Usually I kept more than that but since I knew I was going to the reception earlier, I only brought a small amount of cash along with me.

"Oh, you can't fool me. I know you have some more moolah put up around here somewhere."

"Nah. I don't."

"Go look around here and see what you two can come up with. Tie him up before you go."

The chicks grabbed a black bag that was on the floor, pulled out gray tape, and tied my hands together. One of the bitches went into the dining room and brought back a chair. I was ordered to sit down in it. The taller of the hoes handcuffed me while the other taped me to the seat.

"Man, I don't kno' what the fuck is wrong with y'all but I think y'all, got me mistaken for somebody else." My words went unheard for a while.

"Since you have a big mouth, I am going to fix your problem," the smooth voiced shorter of the women spoke.

She stared into my face with her dark green eyes. She rolled the tape all around my mouth as tight as she could.

"Now, that should keep you good and quiet, Sayveon," she said.

I heard a lot of movement and shit being thrown all around. I wiggled in the chair and moved my hands trying to break free, but it was a waste of time I couldn't budge. I stopped moving and looked over at the one who was in the room next to me. I could see her from where I sat. I moved my eyes up and down her frame to see if I had ever seen her anywhere before, but I didn't know who the hell she was. The taller of the women came in where I was and threw pillows from the sofa set in search of something of value. She slid her hand inside of one of the pillow cushions and quickly tossed it to the floor when she came up empty handed.

"Look, we are not going to play with you. You better tell us where the money is before we shoot you in the ass," the dude walked in and said.

I hunched my shoulders because I was steady telling him that I didn't have nothing in there. The man raised his foot and kicked me in the side. My head dropped and a loud noise from the pain escaped my mouth.

"Urgh," I let out. I tilted my head to the side. I noticed that I could only take shallow breaths. A sharp pain shot through my abdomen that leaned me over.

"Awl. Are you hurting, Sayveon?" the taller of the chicks sarcastically asked.

They all burst out laughing. "Since you like to beat up on women and use them for your advantage, we had to teach you a lesson. My sister isn't your punching bag, and if I ever hear of you putting another hand on her, we will come back and finish you off. You're a douche bag, and you should be dogged around. You don't even deserve to live," the same woman said and slapped me in the face. There was a stinging sensation on my jaw.

"You're a fucking dickhead!" Dude clocked me upside the head with his fist. "Ginger is my goddamn friend. This complimentary ass whopping you're receiving by us has been ordered by her."

Everything went dark, and I blacked out. Guess all of my wrongs had come back on me. There was nothing I could do about it except accept it.

Always Some Bullshit

Sparkle

The ride home with Auntie was a silent one. The only noise was the sound of the gospel music in the background on the radio. My heart had been stepped on, and not only that, but I was also embarrassed as hell in front of Auntie. I was so ashamed that Ontavious had the nerve to bring his li'l girlfriend to church when we hadn't even been broken up for 24 hours.

"Umph, Umph, Umph," Auntie Ruby moaned.

I ignored her because I had a good idea about what she had on her mind. I just wanted the whole situation to vanish in thin air and go away. I continued to drive while I reached over and slightly turned the volume up on the radio.

"I don't know what's going on around here with you and Ontavious. Who was that woman that he brought to church with him?" she pried and turned down the music.

I let out a long sigh. "I would rather not talk about it right now."

"Maybe it would help if you did. Now you know that me and you can have a conversation about anything and it stays between us."

At first my blood began to boil. Then sadness took over, and it took all that I had to keep it together. "When he came over this morning he told me that he is going to build a relationship back up with his ex. He seems to think that I don't appreciate him, but that's not true. I feel like I'm torn between two men. I love Sayveon, and I always will because we share a baby together, but I can't seem to let go of the old things that he's done to me. I was digging Ontavious because he showed me how a woman should be treated and was there for me when I needed a shoulder to cry on. I'll never forget how he was there for me when I was at my lowest point after Sayveon had dogged me out," I vented as I drove back to the house.

Auntie just sat there. I knew that she would understand everything that I said. She was the realest woman that I had talked to in a long time. She kept it one hundred at all times, and I loved her for that. Once I parked and turned the engine off, she began. "You're going to have to choose, and you have to play fair. It's not right to either one of them, and you could find yourself in a dangerous situation. Playing with people's hearts can hurt feelings and get you killed. Everybody isn't strong enough to handle a broken heart."

I shrugged. "I don't know what to do. I don't know if I can ever forgive Ontavious for what he did today by bringing that woman to church. I guess my only other option is to work things out with my baby's daddy."

"Why is Ontavious so hurt? There is a reason that he brought that young lady with him today. It seems like he was trying to make you feel his pain."

I nodded in agreement. "He came to Mama V's party, and I wasn't there. He somehow found me at the hospital with Sayveon. They got into a fight, and he ended up stabbing Sayveon in the butt. He thinks that me and my ex have something going on, but I was only being there for him because his dad got hospitalized." I went on to give her the whole run down of what happened and how Pops made a fool of himself.

"You are going to have to choose the man that gives you a boost and cheers you on when you're at your lowest and has your back. You need to be with someone that you can imagine spending the rest of your life with. Make sure that what you feel is love and not infatuation. Give yourself some time and space from both men and ask yourself what you want from a relationship."

"I want to be loved and to be a wife. I want to be with someone that I can trust and love for a lifetime and have a family and settle down. Maybe I'm a sucker for fairytales, but that's what I am looking for."

"Let love find you. Don't go out searching for nothing. Your life may not be a Cinderella story but you can be happy and live with someone who you love and you two can grow together. Don't give up. Figure out whether you love the person because he is exciting, your sex life is good, or he has the qualities of a future husband. Ask yourself why you care about both of them."

"You're right. I'll somehow figure it all out."

Auntie patted me on the back. "I know it's hard. Make a list of the things you like about them both and the things you don't like. From the list, decide whose negative qualities you don't mind putting up with. It's also a big help if you pick who you share common interest with. Compare how you spend your time with them both and who you are more comfortable with."

"Without even writing it down, I know that Ontavious is who I should choose, but Sayveon will always have a piece of my heart." I rubbed my forehead, took the key out of the ignition switch, and sat there feeling pitiful.

"Take your time and think long and hard on it. Make your final verdict and stick to it. Usually, when in love, you envision how the future looks for your relationship. See who has the most positive characteristics that are positive for a future together. Check into who has a stable plan for his future and is ready to make a permanent commitment. Make sure he'll be a good husband and father if that's what you want. You'll be alright. Pray on it and leave it alone."

I leaned my head back on the headrest and meditated on everything that she had said. I felt that it was time for me to be a woman and choose the man that was best for me. If Sayveon couldn't be faithful to me, then he wasn't the man for me. If Ontavious thought that he could bring another woman to church and I was supposed to eventually take him back, he was wrong. The way that I felt I didn't give a rat's ass if I ended up alone. I didn't deserve that bullshit that they were issuing out. I felt like just rocking it solo for a while and enjoying the single life without all of the stress.

Auntie Ruby opened up the car door and slowly got out and left behind the aroma of her White Diamond's perfume. She was old school and loved that scent. The odor moved by my nose, but I couldn't keep my mind off of Ontavious even though I was upset with him. Auntie grabbed Layla out of her car seat and took her inside. "Don't rush yourself to make a choice. Sometimes when we move to quick, we don't think straight and mess up. Time will help to heal your heart and clear your head. Then you should decide, but don't rush it and never make a decision while you're angry. Think about all that I've said," she said over her shoulder with my baby girl on her hip. She made her way up to the front door, unlocked it, and went on inside.

I grabbed my cell from my purse and dialed Auntie's phone number.

"Hello," she answered. "Don't tell me you've made a decision that fast." She chuckled a bit at her own remark.

"Kind of, but not really. I'll take my time on that right there. I'm gonna take Sayveon his car back. I should be back shortly. Do you want me to get Layla because I don't mind?"

"She's okay right here with me. You just be careful and don't forget what we talked about."

"I won't."

We both hung up and ended the conversation.

The Hangover

Stephanie

The following day I didn't wake up until after noon. I rolled over in bed, let out a loud groan, stretched, and headed to the bathroom. I barely made it to the toilet before I puked inside of it. I had a terrible headache and in desperate need of a Tylenol. I flushed the commode, went straight into the kitchen, and grabbed the bottle of pills. I popped two, fixed a big glass of water, and swallowed them down.

"Shit, I'm fucked up." I was so tired and worn out that I walked into the living room and flopped down on the sofa until I got myself together to take a shower. I noticed a beer can on my end table and a pack of chewing gum that I didn't remember buying. "Damn, I'm bringing shit in here that I don't remember nothing about. I don't even recall having a beer when I got in. I must have been pissy drunk. I gotta do better."

My front door opened and startled the hell out of me. "What in the world are you doing in my damn house, and how did you get in here?" I asked the man.

"You are tripping, hard. We met at the club last night, and you let me crash here. You were faded, so I made sure you got home; then I went to sleep," he said as he sat right next to me like it was all good. He handed me a burger and fries from the McDonald's bag and passed me a cup with some drink inside.

My hand shook, and nervousness took over my whole body. I reached for my coochie. "I hope you didn't fuck me. Did I screw you and I don't remember?" I burst out with, "Oh, Lawd please don't let my pussy be contaminated!" I dropped my head to the back of the couch and slid down to the floor.

"Girl, you're a fool. Hell nah, we didn't fuck. I slept on the sofa. I was too toasted my damn self to be on all that, and plus I didn't have a rubber. I don't fuck new pussy without something on my dick. I ain't trying to go out like that. I mean, you're a cutie and all, but I ain't putting my life on the line for you."

He shot me down, but it was cool, as long as he didn't run up in my drunk ass. I slowly got up and sat next to Tank. We smashed out on the food from Mickey D's; it was good. He chilled out with me for about two more hours, and we talked about some of everything. I enjoyed his company, but I promised myself that I'd never get that tipsy again where I don't remember who the hell is in my apartment. I needed my ass whooped for that.

Return Of The Apes

Stephanie

Tank's and my talk was interrupted when I heard a few loud knocks on the door and the doorbell rang twice. I had a curious look on my face because I hadn't expected any company. Wearing the same dress from the previous night, I walked to the door barefoot and peeped through the peephole. Lo and behold, there were two dummies that I didn't feel like being bothered with.

I opened the door wide and stared them both up and down before asking, "What the fuck do y'all want, and why are y'all here?"

Glenda and her daughter Atasha were standing there. I already knew that they were there for some bullshit.

"You need to open up the door and let us in so that we can talk to you," Atasha spoke. "It's chilly out here." She had on a pair of jeans, a purple t-shirt, and purple and black high-top Adidas. Glenda stood there in black pajama bottoms with a matching shirt and house shoes. She had a black scarf tied around her head. Without make-up, she was uglier than usual. She had dark circles around her eyes and dull looking skin. She looked dehydrated. The heifer needed to drink more water.

"What do we have to talk about? I'm not in the mood for this shit, and I have company right now," I said as I slung the door wide-open.

Glenda peeped around me. "You ain't nothing but a hoe. My son hasn't been in the ground long enough to rot and here you are up in here with another nigga. You been having him stroking yo' monkey and think that you're gonna keep staying here. You gots to go, and I mean now," she spoke and put her hand on her wide hip.

"If you don't get away from my door with this shit, I'm calling the police on y'all ghetto ass bitches," I told them both and started to close the door in their faces. The door stopped. I saw that Atasha had her hand against it preventing it from shutting.

"Get your hand off the door and go on about your business Mama Bear and Baby Bear. Keep on and there are gonna be some problems. You'll be writing a check that your ass can't cash." I tried once again to close the door but this time they both pushed it and I stumbled backwards.

They both invited themselves in; then, Glenda got right up in my face and shoved me backwards. She had Band-Aids all over her arms and a few scratches on the side of her face. "You made me fall from the back of that car yesterday and got me hurting, but I knew I'd get you back." She slapped me so hard across my face that it felt like a bee had stung me. She grabbed my ear and tugged on it as hard as she could. "I'm gonna rip your ear off and stick it up your butt so you can hear me kickin' yo' ass," she threatened.

I heard another knock on the door. That stopped her from touching me. Tank came over and got between us. "Look, I don't kno' what the hell is goin' on with y'all, but you don't need to be putting your hands on her. This is a grown woman. You all should be able to work the situation out without all of this," he said in my defense.

"Boy, shut up and get somewhere and sit down. This doesn't have a damn thing to do with you." Glenda's nose flared, and she gave him a dirty look.

Atasha opened the door and about three black men stood there. "We are ready to get the job started," the oldest man told her.

"What job?" I asked.

Glenda laughed hard, stomped her foot while doing it, and grinned at me. "Baby, you about to be moved. These are my cousins. You must have forgotten that this apartment is in my name. James' credit and yours was fucked up, so he asked me to sign the lease. You are getting up out of here, honey."

"What do you mean?" I was dumbfounded. I never even knew whose name the lease was in because I didn't ever see the paperwork. James kept up with all of that and by me never paying the rent, I didn't have a clue.

Glenda reached in her bra, got a paper, and shoved it to me. I opened it and read where she did sign the lease. I had no other choice but to leave the premises. In the end, she did get the last laugh and left me with nowhere to go.

***

Tank didn't leave me. Instead, he consoled me the entire time mothafuckas were moving and boxing my shit up. There was a huge U-Haul parked outside. About three hours later, all of my stuff was out of the apartment, and there wasn't a thing that I could do about it. I knew that James' credit and mine was bad, so that had to be the reason that he put the place in Glenda's name. I was hurting inside and didn't know what I would do, but I didn't break down in front of that evil woman and her silly daughter.

"Alright, that's all of your stuff," Glenda said as she tossed the last box in the truck. Her cousins jumped in the U-Haul, and the older guy started the vehicle, ready to take off.

"You didn't have to do all of this. I don't know what your problem is, but I'm so tired of going back and forth with you, so I'll be the bigger person and go on about my business," I expressed.

"You don't have another choice, hoe," Atasha broke in.

"You and your mama some snake ass bitches, I'm done with both of you. I gave birth to your nephews and grandsons, and y'all selfish inconsiderate tricks gonna put me out without a place to go to." I stared Atasha down because I was about tired of her slick mouth and how she always tried to back her mother up in her wrongdoing.

She put up her hand. "Whatever. I'm not trying to hear yo' sad story. Go on 'bout your business and get that nigga to find you somewhere to stay."

"Shawdy, don't put me in that right there because I don't have nothing to do with what's going on," Tank told her and placed his arm around my shoulders and led me to his frost-white new modeled Jaguar XJ. "I'm gonna follow you to wherever you're going. Do you have anybody that you can stay with until you get back on your feet, or do I need to get you a room for a couple of nights?" he offered. I couldn't help but dig what he was wheeling. The Jag was a dramatic combination of beauty, luxury, and power, so I knew his money had to be long.

"I think I can find somewhere to go for a while." I hugged him. "Thank you for looking out for me."

"I got you, girl. You seem like you're cool people. I hate to see you in a fucked up situation like this. Hold your head up and don't let it get you down." He reached down in his pocket and got a fat band full of dough. He peeled off two big head hundreds and passed the money to me. "Find you somewhere to take it easy. I'm right behind you and I'll make sure you aight."

I took the cash from his hand. "You didn't have to do that, but I'm thankful. I really appreciate this."

"It's nothing. Get in your car. I'll trail you to wherever you're going."

I went back into the apartment, grabbed the car keys, and went out of the door. I took the apartment key off the ring and tossed it on the ground right beside Glenda's foot. She ran over to me and snatched the whole set of keys from my hand. "You got to be out of yo' mind if you think you're going anywhere in that car," she said.

"Give me my keys back!"

"That car and James' car is in my name too, and I'm giving yours to Atasha," she gladly stated and tossed the keys to her daughter who caught them and dangled the set in the air.

"Yay, I got a new car," Atasha sang out.

One of her cousins walked up and asked for the keys to James' vehicle. She looked over at me. "This cousin right here is going to take up the notes on James' car. See, while you were over here fucking your li'l fuck buddy, I was thinking of a way to get rid of you and bring you down to nothing. Never bite the hand that feeds you."

I tossed my hands in the air. "Take it all. I can always start over. I'm through with you and your family now and I don't ever wanna see you mothafuckas again!"

"Good. 'Cause bitch the feeling is mutual." She and her daughter drove off. I told the driver of the U-Haul to follow me. I jumped in the car with Tank and he drove off. I had the roof over my head and my ride taken in a matter of hours. I had been left with nothing. I went from having something to being without anything. It was a damn shame.

The Struggle

Sayveon

I blinked my eyes several times and realized that the mothafuckas didn't kill me but left me in a fucked up position. I sat in the chair wondering if I'd be found alive or if this was it for me. My side hurt like hell, and it felt like something had been broken. If I survived, I'd have to lock the streets back down and let mothafuckas kno' that I couldn't be dealt like this. I attempted to let out a noise, but the tape over my mouth prevented any sound from coming out. All I could feel was a hard cramp that would come and go on the left hand side.

I slowly moved from side to side to free myself somehow, but it didn't work. There was nothing that I could do. If it happened to be the last day that I lived, I'd have to man up and accept whatever karma planned to give me. I wouldn't bitch up; I'd go out like a G.

My cell phone rang over and over again. I couldn't reach it from where I was. I couldn't have answered it even if I had wanted to. I leaned my head over, hoped for the best, and drifted off. Lately it seemed like I couldn't catch a break for shit.

"Sayveon, are you in there?" a feminine voice called out from the other side of the door waking me up from sleeping.

I mumbled from behind the tape, "Mmm."

A few more knocks came. I knew the familiar voice. It was Sparkle calling out for me and the cell phone rang again.

"Sayveon, if you're in there with one of your hoes just let me kno'. Hell, it ain't like I give a damn. I've been calling your phone, and the hospital said you had been discharged. Let me kno' wassup because I'm beginning to worry about you." The cell beeped letting me kno' that I had a voice message on it. I figured that Sparkle had just left that by the way she talked outside.

"Why do I hear this bastard's cell ringing but he won't answer the door," she quietly said to herself.

"Mmm..." I let out and tried my best to let her kno' that I was in the crib.

"Sounds like you're in there having sex. Nasty motha... Come to the door so I can give you your keys and go on back home. See, that's why I'm glad I'm not dealing with yo' ass no more. You do too much!"

There was a silence. I didn't hear her anymore. I blamed myself for having her thinking that I was laid up with some random broad. The lack of trust is what caused her to think that. I kno' that I had fucked up bad in the past, but now I was in desperate need of some help, and the only thing that she could think of was that I was boning some bitch. I gave up and rested. Every time I moved, the pain from my side gave me hell. I had to have something broken from the way it hurt. It was like something was cracked or bruised real bad.

"Sayveon," Sparkle called sounding closer.

I mumbled as hard as I could. I could hear her footsteps coming toward me, and then she let out a piercing scream when she spotted me sitting there like that. She ran over to me. "What in the world happened to you? Who did this?"

She pulled the tape from my mouth. "Go in the kitchen and grab a knife and cut this shit off my arm," I said with force.

She took off, came back, and sliced it from my hands. My hands dropped down by my waist, and I tried to sit up straight but couldn't from the excrutiating pain.

"What went on in here?" she questioned staring into my eyes with concern and sympathy.

"Some lames ran up on me at the door and did this shit to me. It was all set up by Ginger."

"How do you know that?"

"Because the stupid mothafuckas told me that she orchestrated it. It's war now. I ain't gonna go out like that and let that bitch off easy. She will pay, and I ain't gon' stop until I fuck her up." The anger rose up, and I got madder wit' every minute that went by. I had been crossed by a few niggas but never a bitch. She should have had better sense than to try me.

Now, I'd have to show her what the consequences were to trying to leave my team and be a boss bitch.

Moving On With Life

Stephanie

The ride to where I needed to go was a stressful one. I had time to think and meditate on what I was going through. I always knew that Glenda could be a low down dirty woman, but I never thought that she would take it to that extreme. I couldn't figure out why all of the bad stuff was happening to me. I had cleaned up my act and had been drug-free for some time now. I no longer ran the streets, my two boys and I had a pretty decent relationship now that I had gotten myself cleaned up. That still wasn't good enough for Glenda. She was hurting because she lost her son and taking all of the frustration out on me. She wouldn't stop until she broke me all the way down.

I sniffled a bit and wiped a li'l drop of water from the corner of my eye. Tank looked over at me. "Dry your eyes, babygirl; you'll be aight. You'll come back harder, and you'll make it. Don't let her get you down," he advised.

I nodded. "I'll try not to."

After an hour and a half long drive, we pulled up to my final stop. I just hoped that the person would be generous enough to let me live there for a while until I got my shit together. I had been put in a bad spot, but I shook it off and was determined to keep kickin'. Hell, I had been through much worse, so it was no biggie. I had to woman up and do what I had to do for the time being until I was able to maintain on my own.

I knocked a few times on Aunt Ruby's door, but I didn't get an answer. I figured that maybe my aunt saw the U-Haul parked outside along with an unfamiliar car and decided not to answer. The only sound that I could hear from the front was Layla crying and screaming out to the top of her voice.

"I wonder what the hell is going on up in here?" I said in a low tone to myself.

I knocked several more times and even went to the side of the house and pecked on the window. She still didn't answer for me.

"Auntie Ruby, this is Stephanie. I need you to come open up for me!" I yelled out.

I could feel in my spirit that something wasn't right from the way that the baby continued to holler and cry out. Something inside of me kept telling me that I needed to get in that house no matter how I did it. I walked back to the car where Tank sat. "You cool?" he asked after he let his driver's side window down.

"Not really. For some reason she ain't coming to the door. That's not like her, and I can hear my niece hollering. She's just a li'l baby, so I kno' something is wrong. I can feel it."

"Are you ready for me to unpack this shit or what? I got other places where I need to be," the rude older driver of the U-Haul loudly stated with a forehead full of crinkled frowns.

"I ain't in the mood for your bullshit, so I advise you to shut the hell up before things get real ugly between us out here. I don't kno' where you gotta be but you keep fuckin' with me and you'll end up with a cracked skull. Don't keep on trying me. You and your cousin Glenda can kiss my ass until your lips bleed!" I snapped off.

The man turned his head and got quiet as a church mouse.

Tank murdered his engine, got out of the car, and walked behind as I went to Aunt Ruby's bedroom window and yelled out her name once more. "Aunt Ruby!"

Still there was no response, and Layla's cries were chilling. I grabbed my cell from inside of my purse and dialed Sparkle up. I knew my aunt was home because her car was parked under a portable shed next to her house. The phone rang until Sparkle's voicemail picked up. "Hey, this is Sparkle and unfortunately you've missed me. If you would be kind enough to leave your name, number, and a brief message, I will call you back at a suitable time. Be blessed," her voice spoke on the recorded message.

"I need you to answer the phone because I'm at Auntie Ruby's house and I can't get her to come to the door. Layla's screaming and yelling, and I need to know if you know what the hell is going on. If you don't call me back in a few minutes, I'm going to have to force my way inside because I'm scared that something has happened." I frantically hung up, shoved the cell back down in the handbag, and tossed it to the ground. "Help me find something to burst the window out with," I told Tank.

He grabbed a huge stick from beside an old Pine tree and handed it over to me. "Use this to break it out."

I snatched the long piece of wood from his hand and reared back to hit the glass when my phone rang. I reached down, pulled it out of my purse, and answered. It was Sparkle on the other end of the line. "I just got your message. I'm on my way. Go ahead and see if you can get in the house and see if everything is alright because she never lets the baby cry like that and be careful," she said in a tone full of fear and panic. I could hear the tremble in her voice.

I ended the call and grabbed the stick again and wrapped at the window. Shattered glass flew everywhere. Tank lifted me up, I stuck my feet in first, and he pushed me through the window. I landed on my feet and rushed through the house following my niece's voice until I found her in the living room in her small playpen screaming her lungs out. I then noticed that my Aunt was lying on the floor not moving. I swooped Layla up and calmed her before hurrying to open the front door for Tank and screaming for him to call the paramedics. From the way she laid on her side with her arm propped against the side of her face and not making a sound, I knew that the result wouldn't be a good one.

Pressing For Time

Sparkle

"What's the matter?" Sayveon muffled. I could barely hear what he had asked.

"I don't kno'. Stephanie says that Aunt Ruby isn't coming to the door and the baby is crying. I hope everything is okay. I'm gonna have to go 'cause I need to check on Layla and see if my aunt is alright." I kept my eyes on him because it seemed that he could hardly breathe.

"Baby, don't leave me like this. I feel a sharp pain when I take a deep breath. Go and see about Layla. Call Mama and see if she can get here. I can't stay in here by myself like this." He held on to the side of his ribs.

"I'll do it now."

I called his mom. She answered after a few rings. "Hello, Sparkle."

"Hey, Mrs. Travis."

"Hey there, girl. How've you been? It seems like I haven't heard from you in ages." She chuckled a li'l.

"I'm not doing so good. I am here with your son. A stranger came in on him, and I think he may have some broken or fractured ribs," I informed her and waited for her response.

"Oh, Lawd. That child stays into something. Did he say who the person was that came in? He needs to get you to call the police and press charges on whoever the bastard is."

"He probably won't do that. Do you mind coming over here and staying with him? He may need to see a doctor if he gets any worse." I blew out a long breath of air. Too much was coming at me all at once.

"Sure. Give me a minute to get myself together and I'll be on my way. Leave a key there or something so that I can get in. Lord have mercy, I will sho'ly be glad when my son starts living a better life. He's running up my blood pressure."

"I'll get a key from Sayveon and leave it under the mat at the front door for you."

"Thanks."

"No problem."

"Bye," she said and hung up.

I raced off into the bathroom and rambled through the medicine cabinet until I found him some pain medication. I went down the hall, turned toward the kitchen area, got him a glass of ice water, and came back into the room. "Here, take this," I told him and dropped an Ibruprophen 800 into his hand to keep him from hurting. He slowly held his hand up to his mouth, tossed the medicine inside, and reached for the glass. He was weak as a sheet of wet paper. I held the water up to his mouth and let him take sips until he got the pills down.

"Preciate that," he thanked me.

"No problem. Where are your keys to your house?" I had to lock up before I left. I couldn't leave any doors open because I was afraid that if the people came back, they would kill him.

He pointed over to the sofa. I didn't see them anywhere. I felt down between the cushions, found them, took off the house set, and kissed Sayveon on top of his forehead twice. "I'll turn the alarm on before I leave, and you need to make sure that someone fixes that gate to the entrance. It's been broken for too long and too many outsiders are getting in here," I complained. "Take it easy, and I'll call to check on you, later."

"I love you, Spark," he whispered. 'Spark' was the shortened name that he gave me when we first started dating, and every now and then, he'd still call me that.

Confused about whether or not I should return the love I simply replied, "I kno' you do. I'll call back later to see how you're doing." I put the code to the alarm in which was the year he was born and eased out of the house.

I used the key to lock the top, bottom lock, and then put the key under the doormat for Mrs. Travis when she arrived. When I stood, I heard the sound of a vehicle slowing down and I turned around. A white man drove a dark SUV while a white chick leaned her head out of the window waving a gun. "Tell that motherfucker that it's not over yet!" she yelled at me and fired two shots. Pow! Pow! I dropped to the ground and covered my head. "Next time we're killing him!" I heard the screeching of tires and the vehicle fled away.

I slowly crept up wondering if I'd been injured. A hurting and stinging sensation shot through my left arm. I raised the sleeve of my shirt up a li'l and noticed the skin on my elbow had been taken off and blood spilled out of it. I realized the blood came from me hitting the concrete on the front porch as hard as I did and not from me being shot. "Shit," I said to myself. It ached, but I'd rather have that than a bullet hole. Quickly I grabbed the key from under the front door's mat, used it to open up the house, and walked in.

"Are you okay?" I asked Sayveon who had moved himself from the chair to the leather recliner.

"I'll be a'ight. Where 'dem shots come from?" he slowly managed to question.

"Some fools were hollering out the window and threatening to kill you. They were white folks. Are you beefing with them or something?"

"Ginger's team. She's behind it all," he revealed and slowly looked up at me. "Right now, my mind is on healing, but as soon as I get back right, I'm goin' to war in these streets. I need my heater out of my car. They may decide to come back."

I took off to his car, opened the door, and clutched the burner then ran inside and gave it to him. "You need to go somewhere and chill out for a while until the dust clears. I don't want you to end up getting killed out here. I always told you that these bitches ain't loyal. You fuck these broads, and it never works out between y'all. All they want is your money, and then they're gone to screw another nigga. You gon' learn to listen one of these days."

"Right now ain't the time for this, Sparkle. I feel what you sayin', but I'll be a'ight."

"Cool. I'm gon'."

I got back in his ride and flew off to get to Aunt Ruby's. My phone rang. I reached over on the seat and answered. It was Stephanie. "What's going on?" I wanted to know, worried half to death about my daughter and aunt. When she finished telling me I dropped the phone to the floor and got on the highway rushing back to the country.

More Added Stress

Stephanie

I dropped to the floor and loudly called out Auntie's name. "Aunt Ruby, wake up!"

I looked up at Tank who was on the phone with the paramedics. I gave him the address. "I need you to help me turn her over." He reached over and turned her on her back for me. I let Layla sit on the floor for a minute and put her pacifier in her mouth. Aunt Ruby flinched and held her mouth open. I held her in my arms and promised her that it would all be okay. "You're going to be just fine, my love. Hold on, and it'll all work out."

I checked her wrist for a pulse. She had one. "You want me to lay her in a bed or somethin'?" Tank asked.

"Yes. I don't want her lying on this hard floor."

He placed his arms under her butt and shoulder and moved her body. I put Layla on my hip and directed Tank to her bedroom, and he gently laid her down. She moved her hand and tried to talk but no words came out.

I sat on the bed and comforted Auntie. Tank sat in a chair beside the bed while we waited for the paramedics. All of a sudden, I heard a horn blowing loudly outside. I got up and walked to the door. "What the hell y'all doing up in there?" the U-Haul driver wanted to know with a bad attitude.

I went outside on the front porch. "My auntie is not responding, so we're trying to see about her," I told him.

Ignoring my statement the idiot asked, "Well, what you want me to do wit' yo' stuff. I mean, I got other stuff that I got to do, and you're holding me up."

I moved closer to the U-Haul. "You are gettin' under my skin, and I'm 'bout tired of you. Just unload the bullshit behind the house and when I get time, I'll move it to the storage unit back there. You just a rude, asshole!" I erupted.

"Lady, you're on my damn watch. I'll get this junk unpacked and you can put it wherever the hell you want to," he shot back. He got out and stood there gazing at me with his short, stocky frame and gray beard. He had to be in his late sixties and had little patience. "When you have people helping you, you can't expect for them to wait around all day until you're ready to get started."

"Put it in the backyard, and then get your ass out of this driveway, and if you break anything we'll be in court. I'll sue you," I warned.

He slightly smiled. "If it's broken then that's your problem. You ain't paying me for this."

"Try me." The other two guys got out of the truck. They began helping him take my belongings out and put them outside.

About fifteen more minutes passed before we heard the sound of the ambulance coming down the highway. I went back inside with my niece and waited for Aunt Ruby to get the help that she needed from the paramedics. It had been a long day for me and it seemed that the commotion wouldn't be turned down anytime soon.

Patiently Waiting

Sparkle

First, I had to deal with Ontavious bringing his new bitch to church in front of the whole congregation. Then, it was finding Sayveon tied to a chair and me having to duck to keep from being shot up by some of his rivals. Now, I had to deal with Auntie and her sickness. Stephanie contacted me and told me that some movers were unpacking her and leaving it all in the backyard because Glenda had kicked her out. All I could do was shake my damn head. I told my sister where the storage unit key was out back and I flew to the Madison River Oaks Medical Center in Canton, Mississippi.

At the hospital, I was told to wait in the waiting area until they had more information for me concerning Aunt Ruby's condition. I nervously stayed and hoped that she would be okay. I was exhausted from so much shit coming at me. The bullshit just wouldn't let up on me. As I hung around, I thought about the good times that Auntie and I had shared. She had been a mother to me and the best auntie that I could have ever dreamed of. She welcomed my daughter and me in her home and never acted funny like she didn't want us there. She opened up her home to me and made me comfortable, and she always gave it to me real. Whenever I asked her for advice, she'd give it to me, not sugar-coating anything; then, she would add a sense of humor. I loved that woman, and no one would ever be able to take her place. I admired her wisdom and the way she would guide me through life. I had grown up a lot by just living with her. I learned a lot. Most importantly, I learned to love myself. I was amazed at how I neglected myself for Sayveon.

I'm not saying all women- but most women have little sense of what it means to have love and acceptance for themselves. I'm not talking about loving one's self to the point that they cut everyone off and go into isolation. I once thought that loving myself too much meant that I was being self-centered and not giving Sayveon enough of me. Now I know that not loving me is being selfish. My thoughts have changed, and I am a better person. I think if it wasn't for Aunt Ruby, I probably wouldn't have changed.

I smiled to myself thinking about who I was and who I had become. It was all because of Aunt Ruby. That was my chick and my ace-boon-coon! I came out of dreamland when I heard a voice calling my name. "Sparkle."

I looked up to see the Evans sisters from the church coming toward me. They were the nosiest old women living, and I definitely wasn't hard up for their company. I felt like frowning up and rolling my eyes and telling them to take their old butts home and stay out of our business. Instead, I plastered a fake smile across my face and pretended to be happy to see them.

"Hey, how are y'all doing?" I asked.

"Fine," they replied in unison.

From oldest to youngest, there was Rose, Rosalyn, and Retta. They were fair skinned, and their ages looked to be the late sixties to early eighties. Rose had a silky scarf tied around her head with a li'l silver hair sticking out. She wore a floral dress with white tights and tennis shoes. Rose was the only one with her face made up. There was bright purple eye shadow over her eyes; red lipstick covered her lips, and pinkish blush on her cheeks. Rosalyn and Retta had on long sleeve flannel shirts with black jeans and slide in shoes. All of them had crocheted shawls thrown around their shoulders.

They all hugged me around the neck and Rose planted a wet kiss on my jaw and asked, "How you feelin', Sugar?"

"I'm making it. I'm waiting for someone to come and let me kno' what's going on with my auntie," I said and crossed my legs.

"We heard the siren from down the road. I gotta CB scanner, and I heard the woman say that they had stopped up there at Ruby's house. Later I called and your sister, Stephanie, told me that Ruby was sick and told me what hospital she was in. I called my sisters, and we all rode on down here together," Rose jabbered.

"Well, thank you all for coming," I forced myself to say.

"I would have been here sooner, but I had to finish drying a load of clothes." Rose let out a loud yawn and sat back in the seat. "It's my nap time, but I had to come and check on my church family. Ruby treats us all like we are related. I sure pray that she'll be okay."

I nodded in agreement.

"It's a blessing and a curse to get old. I like being able to see my grandchil'ren and great grandchil'ren, I just don't hardly have the energy to play with them. You'll see what I'm talking about one day. Getting older can give you the blues," she went on to say. The other two sisters laughed and nodded their heads.

"Some days I catch myself with a jar of mayonnaise in my hand in front of the refrigerator and can't remember if I need to put it away, or start making a sandwich," Rose let out and shook her head.

Rosalyn chimed in, "Yes, sometimes I find myself on the front steps of the house and can't remember whether I was on my way up or my way down."

Retta responded, "Well, I'm glad I don't have that problem. Let me knock on wood." She rapped her knuckles on the wooden part of the end table full of magazines and a newspaper. She suddenly looked all around the room as if she was confused and told us, "That must be the door. I'll get it."

It took all that I had not to burst out laughing in her face.

"Retta, I think it's about time for you to check into living in a nursing home. You're the youngest of us all and crazy as a loon," Rose commented and re-directed her attention to me. "Maybe the people here will be able to soon tell you how Ruby's doing back there."

"I'm just thinking positive. Whatever is wrong with her, I think they'll be able to find it. I've heard really good things about this place." I uncrossed my legs and rubbed my forehead. I could feel a headache coming on. "I think I'm about to get a bad headache. My head is hurting so bad."

The oldest of the sisters opened up her purse and took out a few bottles of pills. "I'm a walking medicine cabinet. Do you want a Tylenol, Advil, or Aleve?" She handed the meds over.

"I'll take an Advil, and thank you." I opened the container, placed the top back on, put the pain medication back in her hand, and stepped around the corner to the vending machine. I slid a dollar in, dropped two quarters inside, and pressed the small button requesting bottled water. The water tumbled down. I grabbed it and went back to where the three elderly women took a seat.

The three sisters were discussing a new topic when I sat back down. "Sixty- five is the worst age to be. I always feel like I have to go pee, and most of the time when I sit on the toilet, nothing comes out," the younger one, Retta admitted.

Rosalyn waved her off. "Ah, that ain't nothing, honey. When you're seventy, you can't poop anymore. I take laxatives and eat bran. I sit on the commode all day long for nothing. I can't get a bowel movement to come out."

"Actually, eighty is the worst age of all," Rose broke in.

"Do you have trouble peeing too?" Retta questioned.

"No, not really. I pee every morning at six o'clock like a racehorse. I have no problem with that at all." Rose smiled.

"Do you have trouble taking a crap?" Rosalyn asked with a raised brow.

"No, I sho' don't. I have a BM every morning around six-thirty."

With great exasperation, Retta sat straight up and stared Rose right in the eyes. "Let me get this straight. You pee every morning at six o'clock and your bowels go off at six-thirty. I think you're jiving me."

Rose replied, "I don't wake up until ten."

I had put the pills in my mouth and was taking a sip of water when I spit liquid from my mouth and onto the floor. I laughed until my side hurt. Listening to them talk had cracked me the hell up. Maybe that was what I needed in order to stop worrying myself sick while I waited. Rosalyn chuckled and said, "You're an old shitty and pissy thang then for three and a half hours."

I took the medicine and tried to relax. I did my best not to think about Auntie's current situation. I said a silent prayer. I asked God to watch over her and guide the hospital workers. She needed the best care.

A short time later, the doctor came out of the back area. "Are you the family of Ruby McMurtry?" he asked me.

"I am. These are church members," I spoke back, nervous as hell as to what he was about to tell me. I looked over at the ladies. "Excuse me y'all. I'm going to have a talk with the doctor." I got up and walked over to a corner area.

"Are you her niece, Sparkle?" the black haired, tall, green-eyed Caucasian physician wanted to know.

"I am."

"I'm going to hospitalize Mrs. McMurtry. She has fallen into a diabetic coma. I'll treat her condition with intravenous fluids and insulin; hopefully, she'll come out of it. I've had test done to check her brain for damage, and there is none."

"What caused this?" I knew that she had diabetes, but it had never been a big issue. She'd check it every morning and normally had a good day.

"This is a serious complication that can happen to a person with diabetes who is ill or whose body is stressed. It occurs more in people with type 2 diabetes as opposed to type 1 diabetes. Normally it can take place when the blood sugar gets too high and the body becomes severely dehydrated. This is more common among people over sixty. It may be because older people have an altered sense of being thirsty and are more likely to become dehydrated," he told me in a calm manner.

"I'm glad to know that it sounds like she'll make it."

"She's going to be placed in Intensive Care."

"Can I go see her?"

"Sure. Follow me."

He led the way. I trailed behind wondering what she'd look like when I laid eyes on her. I wasn't used to seeing her sick, only smiling. She always took care of others moreso than herself. I prepared myself to look at her.

Gettin' My Roll On

Stephanie

I had put my niece to sleep earlier in her playpen. I brought the baby monitor outside with me so I could hear her when she got up. After long treacherous hours of stuffing my junk into the large unit with Tank, I was one tired soul. We both flopped downward in two white lawn chairs in the yard and relaxed for a bit. I wiped the perspiration from my forehead and offered him something to drink. I went in, checked the fridge, and found a few ice-cold sodas. After grabbing the sodas, I checked on Layla; then, I went back outside. I handed Tank a root beer, and I popped the top on the grape drink in my hand. I watched him use the back of his hand to remove the dripping sweat that fell from his brow. We had worked up quite a sweat.

"I really want you to kno' that I'm glad that I met you. I wouldn't have ever expected that you would have helped me out as much as you have today," I admitted.

"You're good. Real recognizes real."

"If I'm holding you up from doing anything, you can go on. The hardest part is over. You helped me get done with the biggest part. I'll take my clothes and shoes inside and hang them up in a li'l bit."

"I ain't got shit goin' on. I ain't got a woman right now. I told you, I'm just chilling." He stood and took off his top shirt and left nothing on but his wife-beater. His abs and muscled tummy looked edible. I could have eaten him up for breakfast, lunch, and dinner. Whoa! He moved back down in the seat and looked over at the animals wondering around in the distance. "It's nice and quiet out here. It's like a nice get away from Jack-town wit' all the loud cars, noisy ass kids, and grimey niggas lurking."

"It's goin' to be a big change for me. I'm so used to driving right up the street to get my grocery and household items, but I'm sure I'll get used to it though." I took a few gulps from the can and let out a, "Aahh…"

"Were you raised up out here?" he asked.

"No, I wasn't. I grew up right in Jackson. I would come out here when I was younger in the summer and hang out with my aunt." Switching topics I said, "So, you're single with no kids, huh?"

"I want some li'l shawdys one day, but I'm waiting til' I get wit' the right chick. Then, I'll settle down and maybe have a kid or two. The last broad I was fuckin' around wit' already had two daughters, and her tubes were tied. I had kicked it wit' her for 'bout eight years." He sighed. "I ain't no whorish nigga, either. Don't let the look fool you. My mother died of HIV about fifteen years ago, and I can't shake that shit."

Both of my eyebrows shot up. "I'm sorry to hear that," I sympathized.

"I ain't tryin' to be out here like that. I mean, I have chicks comin' at me er'day, but that ain't nothin' to me. I ain't lookin' for just anybody; I want a wife. Before my mother passed, she made me promise that I wouldn't be sleeping around with random hoes. You can't look at a mothafucka and kno' whether or not they got that package. I see fine ass dymed up females all the time, but ain't none of 'em really on my level. These hoes lookin' for the next come up. I kno' what it's like to pop bands that will make a hoe and her momma do a headstand. Then again, I kno' what it is not to have a dime. I've been in both spots before. I started from the bottom by my damn self, and I ain't tryin' to bring nobody to the top wit' me unless she got her mind right."

I slightly cracked a smile. He had some knowledge on him, and I liked that. He was only thirty-four compared to me being closer to forty, but age didn't really matter. What mattered to me was a man's heart.

"I understand where you're coming from, my nicca," I joked and playfully tapped him on the leg.

He grinned. "Keep on touching on me and you gonna feel somethin' goin' up in you."

I giggled. "Trust, you ain't ready."

"I'm bullshittin' around. I'm tryin' to get to kno' you. All of that other shit will fall in place later on. I ain't in no rush."

I got up. "Well, I gotta go take a shower and head on up to check on my auntie and see if she's okay. My sister sent me a text and said that she was in a diabetic coma and she's about to be moved to ICU."

"A'ight. Keep me up on how she's doin'. I'll send one up for her." He pointed toward the sky meaning a prayer. "Hit me anytime. I'll be around." He wrapped his arm around my waist and pulled me in closer to him. "Be good and get back at me."

"I will," I softly cooed in his ear.

He let go and walked away. Then, he looked over his shoulder. "Do you need a ride up to the hospital?"

I used my pointer finger to show him the two vehicles under Aunt Ruby's shed. "Nah, I will drive one of those up there, but thanks. By the way, do I owe you gas money for driving me all the way out here?"

He chuckled. "You trippin', baby nah. I'm straight." He went on to his car and pulled off.

***

I soaked in the huge white tub before lathering up the towel and soaping my body up with shower gel, rinsing off, and getting out. After drying off, I grabbed a pair of dark blue- skinny-legged jeans and a dark blue Michael Kors long sleeve fitted t-shirt out of the guest-room closet where I hung up all of my clothing. It was the room where I would be sleeping. I reached up at the top, grabbed a pair of all white Nike Air Max, and put them on my feet. Before leaving, I changed the baby and freshened her up. I hadn't had to do that in years, but she was a sweetie and a cutie and I enjoyed it. I picked her up after putting a light jacket on her. Layla giggled and cooed as I talked baby talk to her. "Are you Auntie Stephanie's baby?" She smiled showing off her two front teeth that were trying to come in. "I love you, niecy."

I packed a baby bag, grabbed Aunt Ruby's keys, and walked outside. I laughed to myself when I got to the shed. It was crazy that my Aunt had a gorgeous home but wouldn't invest her money into a more updated car and truck. The car happened to be an old sky-blue '87 Buick Regal with white wall tires. The paint had come off in one spot on the hood, and I could see a piece of cushion sticking out of the passenger side seat. I glanced over at the yellow Ford truck parked beside it, but it wasn't any better. Piled up dirt was under the front tires like she had driven down in the pasture and got stuck in mud. The driver's side door was red, a totally different color from the rest of the vehicle and basically appeared to be barely functional.

"Well, I'll be damned." I stopped and thought for a minute and decided to get in the Buick. There was already a baby car seat in the back. I strapped the baby in and lifted the handle of the driver's side door. It wouldn't open after I had tried numerous times, so I ran over to the passenger side and slid across to get under the wheel. I started the ignition and it started but then cut right back off. I tried several more times, but it kept cutting off so I called Sparkle. "Girl, I'm in this blue car, and it won't start for shit."

"You got to pat the gas three times, and then it'll crank."

I patted the accelerator three times and that baby started right on up. "Okay, thanks."

"You better come on if you want to visit with her," she told me.

"I'm on my way right now."

Driving down the road, I turned the radio on, but no music would come through the speakers. Nothing could be heard but static. I pressed the power button, and it went off. I figured that had to be broken too, like mostly everything else on the car was. It had gotten a li'l stuffy, and I needed some air circulating. With no electric windows, I put my hand over the window roller on the door and tried to roll the glass down. My hand went back and forth, but the bastard wouldn't budge. "Now, ain't this about nothin'," I mumbled.

I pressed down on the A/C button. It seemed that it was the only thing that worked right. Well, until a build-up of dust flew out of the air vents and right up my nose. "What the hell is really goin' on?!!" I jerked the car over, choked, gagged, and wiped my face before heading on back down the road goin' about sixty-miles per hour. Another car coming from the opposite direction met me flashing its lights. I slowed down almost stopping. The older black man let down his window. "Slow that damn car down, turkey!" he insulted.

"Fuck you and don't be bothering me!" I cussed back, mashed the gas, and flew off. I couldn't believe that a man his age would be throwing insults around and he didn't even kno' me like that. "He had to be drunk," I said aloud.

I sped over a hill and BAM! The front bumper swiped the rear-end of a fat wild turkey. The black, overly sized bird with distinct black and white wing feathers limped on to the side of the road. Three baby gobblers trotted out of the grassy field and sprinted behind the mother crossing the highway. I felt bad that I had gon' off on the old man and he was only warning me about the turkey ahead. I slowly pressed down on the gas pedal and eased off. It had been the silliest car ride of my life.

Comin' For Me

Sayveon

I heard lots of movement at the front entrance. I grabbed a hold of the burner and held on to it firmly, ready to let off some rounds. Then I heard the voice that I had known all of my life.

"Sayveon, are you okay, baby?"

A key went inside of the keyhole, and in she came with open arms and eyes full of tears. "Yeah, I'm good, Mama. Glad to see you."

She gave me a big hug around the neck and kissed my cheek. After hugging, she placed her hand on her hip and a finger in my face. Before she even started, I knew what time it was. "You are going to have to do better than what you are doing. You are going to keep right on until somebody shoots the shit out of you if you don't change your life around. You're headed down a road of destruction, and the devil is the driver. God can't bless you if you continue to live like an ole' thug. Can't you see that this is going to get you put in a graveyard somewhere?" she fussed.

I hunched my shoulders. "I kno' it, but you can't judge me. Nobody is an angel. I'm goin' to get it right one day," I said in a low tone.

"Why not get it right today? Tomorrow isn't promised and yesterday is gone."

"I feel you and all that you talkin' 'bout, but we better be gettin' up out of here. I need to stay at your crib for a minute and stay out of sight until I figure some stuff out."

"That's what I was goin' to say to you, too. You can't be here by yourself. It's too dangerous. Do you think maybe you should get checked out to see if anything is broken?" she asked as she raised the side of my shirt up. "Goodness boy! You got bruises all up and down your side."

"I doubt if I got something broken. Just need to get somewhere and rest. Time will heal the rest."

Mama helped to get me some clothes to wear. She put them in the car before coming back to help me out of the house. With her help, I lifted myself upward, hobbled to her whip, and got in. After she helped me into the car, she went back, set the alarm, and locked up. When she drove away, I glanced back at the place I called home and knew that I could never go back there to live. It was a wrap and now a part of my past.

Mama pulled into a Shell gas station up the street. "I got to go in here and get me a Coke to drink. You know that's my soother when my nerves get bad as hell. Do you want anything back?"

"I'm cool. You go on ahead. I'll be a'ight until you get back."

Mama got on out and went into the store. A dark colored van drove up, and it kinda shook me because I now had to stay watchin' my back. An elderly white dude got out wit' a cane. He nodded his head at me and crept on inside of the gas station. My cell began to go off. I looked down and saw Ginger's number on the caller ID. The bitch's ego was on swoll, but it would all be brought down when I caught her.

"Bitch, I'm gon' come for you! You sendin' yo' people to handle yo' business, but I ain't one of them clowns you used to fuckin' wit'. I ain't trippin; I'ma rock up wit' my fam and show you I'm one hunnid in these streets," I went off.

She laughed as hard as she had ever laughed in my ear. "Sayveon, you aren't going to do shit. I have a team that will put holes all through you if you're ever caught in my vicinity. The war is on, so let the best girl or guy win," she said back.

She threw me off because she never had heart like that before. A li'l money and a few soldiers on her side and she was bossed up and ready for whateva. I gave her a piece of the game but never gave up er'thang that I knew. She took the li'l knowledge that I had dropped on her and took off wit' it. Really, when I thought 'bout it, the shit was funny that a white girl from the suburbs thought that she could go up against a hustler like me who had been running shit for years. She was an amateur tryin' to play the role of a real goon.

"Bet that." I hung up. My reputation spoke for itself I wasn't gonna tongue wrestle wit' her. Actions always spoke louder than words.

When I glanced up, I could see Mama and the old white man coming out of the store and making their way to their vehicles wit' bags in their hands. The older dude crept at a turtle's pace, trying to make it along. All of a sudden, I heard the sound of a loud gunshot. I turned and saw a dark colored SUV rolling by with its driver's side window down. The white male driver had a white towel covering his face. He pointed the iron toward my direction and started bustin'. I grabbed my glock from my waist. Wit' all the strength I had in me, I hopped out of the car and fired back. Mama ducked for cover, and the SUV sped off. I heard Mama hollering and screaming out, "Oh, Jesus, please somebody come and help!"

It took me sometimes because of my pain but I made my way over to where she was. Mama was on the ground and her loud screams pierced through my ears. Another innocent victim had gon' down.

Popped In Broad Daylight

Sayveon

As soon as my feet made it in front of the car, I could clearly see the scene. The old man lay sprawled on the ground on his back. The shots had popped him in his dome piece and left a hole on the side of his head. His thick black-framed eyeglasses had fallen off his face and were lying beside his head. Blood stained his blue jean overalls and white shirt. Mama held his head in her soft hands.

"This ain't right," Mama murmured softly before bursting into tears. Blood covered her own clothes. She was bathing in it, but she didn't care at all. There was another wide hole in his chest. His bloody fluid leaked out of it. I knew from looking at him that he was dead. Mama tried to hold his arm up, but it fell as if his muscles had turned into a block of ice.

A crowd gathered outside of the store and people gawked at the dead body lying in my mother's arms. A short black older woman yelled out from her car, "Has anyone called for help?" She got out of her car and walked over.

"Nah," I said.

"Well, we can't stand around and not do nothing. Time is important right now. This man needs some help." She used her phone to call up a medical team. In no time, police cars swarmed the building. A black female officer walked over and started pushing people back in order to secure the scene. The paramedics arrived and soon a medical team took over. They asked Mama to let them try to see if he had a heartbeat. One medical person checked the side of his neck with a pair of blue gloves covering her hand. She shook her head 'no' at the other member of her crew letting him know that there was no pulse.

The black officer and other police began questioning everybody in the parking lot and inside of the store. Yellow tape was placed all around the area, and no one was allowed to come in or leave out. The female police officer started with me. "Sir, what happened here today?"

"All I kno' is that a SUV drove by here shootin'. I didn't see the driver, only the whip that they pushed. I can't tell you nothin' else 'cause that's all that I saw," I hurried and said. I was tryin' to make it clear that I didn't want no parts of that.

"Did you get a view of the license plate?"

"No."

She wrote down my statement on a sheet of white paper and asked for all of my contact information. She looked over at Mama. "Ma'am, I need to know what you saw."

"I told my son that I was going to go inside to get something to drink. The old man came in right after I did. I got my Coke, and then I went over to the ATM machine to get some money out. We walked out of the store at the same time. When I was almost to the car a man in an SUV drove by, pointed his gun at us, and started shooting. He was a white man, but he covered his face with a towel. I could see another person on the other side of him, but I don't know if it was a man or a woman," she said and began to cry. "I have never in all of my life had to witness anything like that before."

The woman nodded. "I understand, ma'am. I know it's hard, but try not to get upset and tell me as much as you can about the shooter."

"That's all that I saw. I dropped down to the ground when he shot and covered my head."

"Thanks so much for your help. Now, I'll need to get your name and some information in case we need to contact you or call you down for questioning."

Mama gave the officer her info and she thanked Mama before walking away to talk to another officer. A white coroner's van wheeled in and parked while the detective and officer went back and forth over what happened from the police report.

The old man's skin color began to slowly change to a light purple. The detective took photos from every angle. He finished with the pictures, and the coroner placed the body in a yellow body bag and zipped it up. The two of them placed the deceased on a stretcher, and he was sent off to the County Examiner's Office.

"You and your mother can leave, but if you have any other information for us, don't hesitate to call the office," the detective said. He handed his business card to Mama, and we got in the car and left. The ride to Momma's house in Crystal Springs was a quiet one. The shock of what she had seen had her spooked.

The Troubling News

Stephanie

I found the waiting area, but by the time I made it, Sparkle told me that visiting time was over. No one could go back and see her again until the visiting hours came back around. The huge round clock in the waiting room let me know that it was fifteen minutes after three o'clock. I took a seat next to Sparkle to wait. I bounced Layla up and down on my lap and watched her giggle and scream out in fun.

"She sure is a beautiful baby," one of the church members, Rose complimented.

"Thank-you," Sparkle responded.

"Not trying to get in your business, but weren't you dating Ontavious at one time? He's such a sweet young man," Rose pried, leaning her head slightly to the right waiting for a response.

"Yes, we did date for a while." I could tell that Sparkle got uncomfortable when she cleared her throat and then looked away.

"Well, who was that other woman that he brought to church with him on Sunday?"

"Maybe she was a friend of his. I don't really know, and to be honest, right now I don't even care. What he does is on him. We aren't together anyway." Sparkle folded her arms across her chest.

"One thing that I have learned is that you sho' can't cry over spilled milk. I thought ya'll made a gorgeous couple and would have gotten married. He's such a handsome young man, and he seems to love the Lord and care about people."

The other two sisters agreed by saying Um, hmm…

The middle sister Rosalyn added her two cents. "You young girls better be glad that I can't go back to my early twenties. I woulda got with that young nice looking man and rocked his boat." She got so tickled behind her comment that her stomach jiggled when she laughed.

Sparkle and I looked at one another and thought it was funny too.

"I would have rocked his boat and water too," Retta said. She paused for a moment before asking, "Who are we talking about again?"

Rose shot her a dirty look and shook her finger at her. "Chile, you gon' have to go to your doctor and tell that man to give you some 'Old Timers' medicine before you lose yo' mind." Rose leaned over in Rosalyn's ear and tried to whisper, but she could still be heard. "She's gettin' worse by the day."

Retta poked her lip out and frowned. "There ain't a damn thing wrong with me, you old two-faced woman. Don't whisper about me. Be bad enough to say it to my face. Because you're the oldest don't mean shit to me. I bet I can remember how to give you my ass to kiss."

"Mind your manners, woman," Rosalyn told Retta and tried to calm the situation down. "You know better than to use that foul language in front of these young ladies. You ought to be ashamed of yourself," she lectured.

"Don't tell me how to act. You should be shame that I saw Pastor Wilson pulling up in your yard last night. It's a lot that I know so don't think that I have Alzheimer's." Retta looked her sister Rosalyn up and down and batted her eyes before turning her head away.

"It's not a crime for him to come to my house."

Rose cut in- "You don't have Alzheimer's. You got 'Old Timers.' You're *old*, and it's about *time* you get some medicine to help you with your memory."

"Don't mess with me, Rose!" she shot back and jumped back to her conversation with Rosalyn. "I saw the preacher when he drove up and he stayed over there for hours," she revealed and everyone had shocked faces.

"Kno' your facts before you start spreading rumors. He came over, and we prayed for our members who were sick and shut in. I asked him to have a plate of dinner; he ate, and then went on back home. It was no big deal."

"Oh, well he must have prayed in your bedroom. I was looking dead at you when you closed your blinds and turned the light off with him standing right up behind you."

"Well, I'll be damned," Rose softly said.

All three of the Evan sisters lived side by side and had been since I was a li'l girl. The room grew silent for a while. The only sound came from Layla's mouth playing and cooing. Soon they told us they were leaving, and all stood up.

They all gave us hugs and kisses and began walking out of the door. We overheard Rose tell Retta, "You didn't have to put your sister's business out there like that in front of those young women. You could have talked to her about that in private."

"The truth is the light," Retta shot back and continued out of the building.

Rosalyn re-routed and made a u-turn back over to us. "You all have to excuse my sister, Retta. We think that she has a bad case of memory loss, and now I'm starting to think that her mind is playing jokes on her. Don't let what she said go any further. I'm an active and faithful member of the church. I grew up there. I would hate for this to get out and make me look like a whore. It's simply- not true," she explained.

"You have our word that it won't get out by us," Sparkle promised.

When they all were gone, we burst out in laughter. Those three made me forget all about the chaotic day I had and brightened it up some. Now, my only worry was Auntie. I wanted her to pull through and be able to come back home.

"I've had some good times with Aunt Ruby. I don't want anything to go wrong with her," Sparkle said and looked down at the floor.

I rubbed her back. "God will work it all out. There's nothing else for us to do except pray. We have to continue on and make sure that she gets taken care of properly while she's here, but I have a feeling that everything is gonna be alright," I assured. My sister sat there silently. Our aunt had been a big help to us both, and I couldn't imagine life without her.

***

By the time Sparkle and I made it back out to Aunt Ruby's house, we were both exhausted. I went into the bedroom and laid across the bed, wondering how my life would turn out. My thoughts wondered back to my boys and how much I loved and adored the both of them. They were doing so well, and I really wanted to continue to make them proud of me. I'd have to go out and eventually get a job so that I could support myself. Without James' income, I had no money, and there was no way in hell I could survive without that.

I was deep in thought when I heard Sparkle talking loudly. I hadn't heard anyone come in, so I figured she was on the phone. I eavesdropped and assumed that it was Sayveon when she said, "Nigga, I ain't got no talk for you. You can keep doing what you're doing and I bet I'ma be a'ight."

I figured that she had hung up on the person when I no longer heard her talking. I heard knocking at the front door and walked to the living room to see who it was. I heard the sound of plates and water running in the kitchen and knew that my sister was washing dishes and apparently hadn't heard the knocking.

So I walked over and opened up the door. There stood Ontavious. Sparkle had already told me on the way home about how he handled her at church with his new *Sweet Thing*. My nose flared, and I said, "I don't think my sister wants to talk to you after the way you shitted on her at church. You have a lot of nerve to pop up here like this. Where's your new woman?"

He held his hand up like he didn't want to hear what I had to say. "I'm not here for all of that. One of the members of the church called and told me that your aunt had to be rushed to the hospital. I came over out of concern."

"Hmph, really?" I wasn't convinced at all.

"Ask your sister to come to the door. I would like to talk to her."

"Nope. You can't dog her out and expect to come over here like it's still good. She liked you a whole lot, and you treated her like she was some gum on the bottom of your damn shoe. Y'all men need to recognize a good woman and learn how to treat her because if you don't know there's someone else out there that does," I sermonized.

Sparkle walked up behind me and said, "Preach." My niece had also crawled up to us and was on the floor looking up at all of us. I picked her up and planted her on my wide hip.

"I need to speak to you in private," Ontavious told her.

She shook her head in disagreement. "Hell, nah. You came dragging that thang up in church with you like you were really on top of your game with your li'l trick beside you. But thanks for showin' me the real you. You're flaky, and maybe you aren't the man that I need to hold me down. Get the fuck away from here before I jaw yo' ass!" she snapped.

"Tell him, sis. Don't let him get away wit' that sheisty shit," I co-signed standing behind her.

She turned to me. "Don't worry I got this."

"Why are you even in our business? Let me talk to her and she can say what she needs to say to me, alone. I'm not here for you. I'm here for your sister," he let me know in a snobbish manner.

"Oh, don't get sideways wit' me because I'm not the one-"

Sparkle put her hand on my shoulder. "Hol' up. I'll step out here and see what he has to say. Relax because this shouldn't take but a hot second."

"Let me know if you need me," I said. I gave Ontavious a long hard stare before I turned and walked to the kitchen to make the baby a warm bottle and put her to sleep for the night. I knew my sister was strong enough to make her own decision on whether or not she wanted to continue their relationship. So, I stepped back and let her be. After being involved with Sayveon all of those years, I had no second guesses on whether or not she could hold her own.

Another Bobblehead

Sparkle

The sun had gone under and darkness began to take over the sky. We stood right next to Ontavious' ride and behind Sayveon's black whip. I let out a long sigh from annoyance, and plus I was hot as a jalapeno pepper with him and his dumb shit. Out of all niggas, I never expected him to show his black ass and try to get down on me the way that he had. Ugh, I had had it with the extra bullshit when it came to men.

I leaned my back up against his truck. "I'm listening. Go ahead and say whatever it is that you need to get off of your chest."

"Actually, there's a lot that I need to let out. I went to the party to be with you and show my support as your man. When I couldn't find you inside, I asked Mama V where you were and she told me that a family member of yours had an emergency and had to be taken away by ambulance. Out of concern, I asked her what hospital, but she claimed she didn't know. I went outside and asked a Spanish guy if he knew what hospital the person in your family had gone to, and after he went back in and asked around, he came back and told me that Al was the Baptist Hospital."

I stopped him. "You should have called my phone, and I would have found a way to come back and be with you. I would have never wanted you to come up there and end up boxing wit' my ex. I'd never want to see you hurt."

"Let me finish. I came up there to make sure that you and whoever your family was, was okay. Your phone kept going to voicemail and it had me worried about you."

Maybe he's right about my phone because sometimes I can be in a bad area and get no signal and besides; he has no reason to lie. "I'm fine with all that you just said, but you assumed that I had fucked him or something. He is my daughter's granddad, and I only went to make sure he was okay. Sayveon asked if I would come. Yes, now that I look back at it, I was wrong, but I didn't see it as anything but taking a ride."

"Sparkle, that's not a good excuse. After all that you've gone through with him going somewhere with him should have been the last thing on your mind. I showed you how it feels to be embarrassed, disappointed, and hurt." He patted on his chest while saying, "I'm a man, but I have feelings and you can't dish out what you're not willing to accept. Out of spite and disappointment, I spoke back to my ex and asked her to go with me on Sunday," he explained. "Men have pride, and as my woman, you shouldn't have tampered with that. I have to be able to say you're mine and hold my head up."

He reached out for me. "Don't touch me. I need time. You should never assume something because things aren't always the way that they look."

"You're right. Understand this, I'm an optometrist, and I could have been thrown in jail that night for scrapping with your ex-boyfriend over some bullshit. I've never put myself in that situation before, and I have never dealt with a woman that has ever had me tied up in that kind of shit. Either you're mine, or you're not. If you were mine, I wouldn't have had to be out there swinging with a thug. I put a promise ring on your finger and promised to be yours. I wasn't bullshitting around when I did that."

I stood there zoned out. I felt bad because I had gotten myself in a sticky situation. All I did was go to Mama V's party and somehow my old feelings for Sayveon crept back up and caused me to hurt Ontavious. I felt about as low as hell is from heaven.

The view of car lights pulling up caused us both to look up. The car turned into the driveway, and the headlights shined directly in both of our faces. The car came to a complete stop. The driver's door opened. I saw a woman's heel hit the ground before she stepped out and whipped her long hair out of her face.

"You told me that you were coming to check on the next door neighbor and see if everything was okay. You didn't tell me that she lived over here. I've been calling your phone, and you aren't answering. Tell me what the hell is going on here." The same woman that he came to church with had the nerve to pop up where I stayed, running up behind Ontavious.

"I didn't need you to come here checking up on me. I'm having a conversation with her right now, and I'll be back when I'm done," Ontavious said to her.

She flicked her hair from her eye again and popped her fresh-coated red lips. She looked to be a bougie broad. She had a well-kept physique, kinda on the thick side with a juicy butt. It didn't intimidate me because I was a walking coke-bottle with an ass so phat, I could give a nigga a heart attack. So, I was so not sweatin' the chick.

"Well, I'm not leaving until you leave. That's just what it is." She posted up beside the car and began tapping her pedicured nails against the hood.

I glanced at Ontavious. He knew me well enough to know that my patience was wearing thin and I had 'bout had enough of the whole situation. Besides, I was beginning to feel disrespected by her coming to the house with that nonsense. "Look, you better check this bitch and let her know that she's a few seconds from getting that ass tagged," I warned him, but saying it to them both.

"Camryn, go on, and I'll be there in a little bit because we're going to have to sit down and have a serious conversation anyway." He went over and opened her car door. "Go ahead, and get in and I'll be there shortly."

"No," she refused.

I cleared my throat and balled up my lips because the fury began to take over and put me in beast mode. "Trick, if you don't get your ass out this yard I'm gon' beat you until I get tired. Now, I don't kno who the fuck you think you are to be comin' up in here like you regulating shit, but you 'bout to make me fold you up," I let her know.

"I'm not worried." She blew me off in her li'l tight fitted dark-colored pants suit with a white shirt underneath thinking she was Miss America.

"Get your li'l prissy ass off your car and haul ass," I said.

"Nope." She stood there like she wasn't worried 'bout shit I had said. There's nothing I hated more than a rude bitch.

"Calm down, baby. Let me get this straight with her," Ontavious said to me and stepped up closer to her. "You're going to have to leave here. Better yet, don't even worry about me anymore. I tried to get over my ex by hooking up with you, but it's not going to work between us. No hard feelings, and I apologize for playing with you like that," he told her.

Her hand rose and connected to the right side of his jaw. He pinned her arms down, and she wiggled and kicked and screamed out, "You no good, asshole!" She then leaned forward and I heard him holler out in pain. The stank hoe had her teeth sunk into the skin of his neck. Ontavious rapped her across the face with a bitch slap that stopped her from biting him.

"I've had enough of you," I said to her. "C'mon." I swung the first lick bangin' her in the head with my fist. She fought back, and we both were going head up, blow for blow. I kept right on beating on her skull. I held her head with one hand while puttin' in that work with the other. Two long black tracks fell out of her hair, and the more I hit and pulled, the more I found out how baldheaded the whore was. Weave flew everywhere. I began to drag her by her hair and we both tumbled to the ground. She climbed on top of me.

"I'm busting you in your shit the same way you did me. Don't- ever- put- your- hands- on- me, bitch," she said while punching me with each word that she spoke. She nailed my hands down with her knees and socked me in the face.

Ole' girl wasn't as stuck up and prissified as I summed her up to be. She had a li'l fighting game on her. I moved and pushed upward until I got her off me. Ontavious got in between us to break it up. It didn't work. I ran around him, and we locked up again. I jerked her by her few weave pieces that still survived the battle that she was in, and she toppled to the ground. I got on top of her, sat my ass on her chest, and beat her face in. Bam! Bam! Bam! The hard licks bonded with her nose. Blood oozed down like a leaky faucet and rolled down her chin.

Ontavious pulled me off of her, and she got a chance to kick me in the stomach. "Oh, hell nah. Put me down!" I hollered and screamed.

Stephanie ran outside. "Who is this bitch you out here fighting?" she asked me with a confused expression. Her head went back and forth from me to Camryn.

I huffed and puffed. "This dirty trick came in the yard for Ontavious. It's the same one that came to church with him."

Camryn hopped up from the ground and tackled me when Ontavious let me go. I fell down on my ass, and we rolled all over the grass. Stephanie came up and kicked her so hard that she knocked Camryn off me. She laid there panting and holding her chin. "Stay up off my mothafuckin' sister!" Stephanie shouted.

The large pecan tree that Camryn laid by had something by it that made me want to smile. When I heard her go, "Ouch!" I knew that the large ant pile was all over her. She jumped up and shook her clothes to get the small insects off her. She skipped and hopped all around as if she was on fire and screamed out as loud as she could.

"Uh, huh those ants got a hold of your ass," Stephanie said to her with a smirk on her face.

Camryn patted her head and shook it from side to side to shake the crawling insects out of it. Finally she took off to her vehicle and sped out of the yard like a mad woman.

Ontavious touched my arm. "Are you okay?"

"You know what? Fuck you. You had her at your house, but then you wanna ask me to come outside and talk to you. I thought you were different, but you ain't no better than who I had before you!" I snatched away and started toward the house.

"Baby, I choose you."

"Choose to leave me the hell alone!"

"Do you want me to stop by tomorrow and feed the animals for you?" he asked as I walked off.

"I don't want you to do shit. I'll get it done."

"Baby, stop being stubborn. You don't know anything about feeding those horses and cows. Let me come over tomorrow and make sure it is done. You can watch me, and then you'll know how to do it yourself."

"Go straight to hell."

I walked in the house, and Stephanie came behind me. She locked up the house as I took a seat in the living room. I glanced over at Layla sleeping peacefully with her pacifier in her mouth. Her daddy sure wasn't the best man in the world, and we had our bad times, but if I wanted to be a part of nonsense, I could have stayed with him and kept putting up with his fuckery. I just wanted to take a long hot shower and start over fresh without all of the negativity. How dare Ontavious have that woman at his house and then come to see me. Yeah, he told her that it was over, but I still hurt inside. Hopefully a good night's rest would help me to sort things, and maybe tomorrow I will be able to think clearly.

Bringin' The Heat

Sayveon

Sparkle had let me and Mama kno' that her and the baby were good. She tol' me 'bout her Auntie and what happened too. I never had the chance to meet her Aunt Ruby when we were together, but I knew she had to be cool as a fan to even let her and Layla be there wit' her. I missed my li'l Princesses, and as soon as I healed and got myself back right, I would go and visit wit' them or either have a li'l sleepover when I got situated. I loved my seeds regardless of what I went through wit' the mamas. I leaned back on the bed in my old room at Mama's crib and put my head against the wall. I had shit that had to be taken care of. I reached for the cellie on the short wooden table by the lamp and dialed up a number.

"What up, Cuz?" Menace, cuzzo from Memphis spoke. I hadn't seen him since he came to The Sipp and I got popped at the club that night wit' Carmen, but we still chopped it up from time to time.

"Chillin' at my mom's crib. A lot of shit jumpin' off over here. It's gettin' hectic, fam. I got mothafuckas comin' at me from all kind of ways. You kno' what time it is though."

"Gotcha. I'll holla at you. I got a few thangs I need to wrap up on this end before I bounce that way. I gotta see what's up wit' the trees, anyway. I'll get wit' Dez on the business tip. It's dry out here, mane. So, I kno' I can do some grindin' and flippin' and make a killin'. Nah mean?"

"I feel you. Be easy out there, my nigga. Deez fools thirsty. I just had a bitch send for me, nigga. Had her people run up in my crib and shit."

"Dayum, those Sipp chicks gettin' down like that over there?" he asked and chuckled a bit. I heard a feminine voice in the background tell him that somebody wanted to holla at him for a second. "A'ight Cuz, I'll get at you."

"That's what's up."

I hung up. No doubt, I missed my boy Rich. We would kick it together, and he wasn't afraid to lay a nigga down. I hated that it happened the way that it did between him and Pops, all over a bitch that wasn't shit. I understood where Pops mind was at the time. Loyalty Over Everything was what Pops lived by. That's why I had to make sure that he never found out about Carmen and me, but I felt that it was a dead and squashed situation.

I grabbed the remote from on the bed and turned on the television. The ten o'clock news report was on. The young, black anchor said, "On the news tonight police are on the hunt for a gunman in a dark colored SUV who opened fire on a North Jackson gas station, killing a seventy- two year old man in cold blood. Alexis Champion is live tonight; I'll turn it over to you, Alexis."

The screen split between the black anchor and the young white chick, Alexis, and she spoke holding the microphone in front of the Shell station. "Katrina, police say they still don't have a description of the shooter who shot and killed the elderly gentleman here right off of Old Canton Road. The shooting happened right behind me earlier today and that's leaving residents fearing for their lives."

The camera crew interviewed a Vietnamese man. "This has shocked me. This is the first time that I have ever heard of something like this happening on this side of town."

The attention went back to Alexis. "Police and crime scene tape surrounded the station. Police say the elderly man was shot around two o'clock this afternoon and died on the scene. As police look for clues, neighbors wonder why such a horrific crime took place right here in an area just blocks away from their homes. Authorities will look at several surveillance cameras on the premises and are asking anyone with any information to call the number at the bottom of the screen. Reporting live tonight from WJTV 12, I'm Alexis Champion."

I turned the TV off and decided to go to sleep. The Ibuprofen pills that Mama brought from my crib had me sleepy as hell. Right before I drifted off, Mama tapped on the door and peeped her head in. "I came by to check on you. Are you okay?"

"I'm a'ight."

She came in and sat at the foot of the bed. "You kno' you're my baby and I love you to death, but I want you to do the right things and ask for forgiveness. None of us is perfect, but we all need some perfecting. Whatever it is that you've gotten yourself into, you better get it right with The Good Lord and ask him to clear this mess up. I think that those people were after you again today and that poor old man got caught in the crossfire."

"Mama that could have all been a big coincidence. People shoot up places all the time. Don't upset yourself wit' that right there, and I got me. It'll all work out," I assured.

"I hope so. Goodnight and sleep tight."

"Love you, old woman," I teased.

"Boy, please. I still got it."

She turned off the light, and I went off to sleep. The following weekend couldn't come fast enough.

An Unbroken Bond

Sparkle

The first bit of morning arrived and the sunshine streamed through the curtains. I laid under the crumpled quilt and my eyes slowly blinked open. Deep grunting noises escaped my mouth as I twisted my back and stretched my neck. Casually I glanced over at the alarm clock, stared at the ceiling, flipped the pillow, and yawned. My nose twitched and caught the faint fume of sizzling bacon and a hint of maple syrup drifting from the kitchen. I bunny-sniffed again, and that time I was positive, certain, and sure that breakfast was being cooked. My stomach growled, and I could picture li'l white grease bubbles in a black frying pan.

Standing up and opening the blinds, I could see the stunning display of orange, gold, yellow, red, and tangerine rays dancing across the sky and over the tops of the highest trees and into the window. The sound of the cackling hens, cows mooing, horses making a 'neigh' noise, and birds chirping was the usual farm music that I had gotten used to hearing. I peered over in the baby crib. Layla slept on her side with her pacifier glued to her lips. I followed the scent and found Stephanie sitting down at the small kitchen table sipping on hot tea. She had a breakfast plate in front of her with eggs, grits, bacon, and toast on it. She put the mug down and ate a mouthful of eggs.

"Good morning li'l sis," she greeted with her eyes stuck to the newspaper in front of her.

"Hey girl. I see you got up early and cooked. I'm glad too because I ain't had shit on my stomach since yesterday evening but my hand."

I saw the food sitting on top of the stove, so I grabbed a plate, filled it up, and joined her at the table. "I went ahead and got on up. Damn cows hollering and chickens clucking around here. I couldn't sleep hearing all of that. I got to get used to this shit," Stephanie complained and slowly drank a few sips of her drink.

"It'll get better."

"I'm looking at this paper and an old man got shot to death right over there by where Sayveon lives. His name is Robert Stovall. It's saying that his only child is trying to come up with burial money. She's asking for help to bury him. Now, that's sad."

"I wonder what happened. That's normally a pretty quiet area."

"A gunman fired shots out of a ride, and the man got hit and died instantly."

"These people are looney. It's not safe to go anywhere now-a-days."

I could only imagine how that poor daughter must have felt knowing that her elderly father was killed in cold blood. I wondered how Pops and Aunt Ruby were doing for a minute. They both were older people and both were sick and trying to recover. I'd have to call the head nurse and check on her later in the day.

She needed me more that she had ever needed me before and I intended to be there for her.

***

US- 51 South had cars bumper to bumper. I believed it was because of the lunch hour traffic. I traveled to Crystal Springs to return Sayveon's car. Stephanie followed behind me in my Infiniti. After a long drive, we finally made it to Crystal Springs. I found Mrs. Travis' house, parked on the side of the street, and got out with my daughter. Stephanie came behind me.

"Hey there." Mrs. Travis met us at the door and invited us in. She wore a pink jogging set, and her hair was covered with a scarf.

"Hello, how are you doing?" I asked.

"Chile, I'm making it." She took Layla out of my arms and kissed her juicy jaw. "Hey, li'l girl. You are a cutie pie. Lookin' like, Sayveon." She told us both to have a seat.

"Mrs. Travis, this is my sister Stephanie," I introduced.

They greeted one another. "I just finished up in the kitchen. I did a big dinner. Y'all better have some," she offered.

"No thank you," we both said.

"Y'all might wanna think twice about it. I did some cornbread dressing, collard greens, potato salad, fried okra, and macaroni and cheese. The sweet potato pies are still in the oven but should be ready pretty soon."

Listening to her name all of that good soul food almost made my mouth water, but I still refused.

"Sayveon was back there resting in his room earlier. If you want to, you can go back there and talk to him," she said to me.

I was on my way to the back when he met me in the hallway. "What's up, babygirl?"

"What's going on?"

"Nothing. Back here watching TV and chilling. Where's my li'l girl?"

"In there with your mom."

He went up front and a huge smile came across his lips. "Daddy, baby!" Layla turned her head around and looked at him. He swooped her out of his mother's arms, and his face lit up with joy. Sayveon snuggled his nose into her cheek, and she held her mouth open and gummed on his face with her wet mouth. "Ugh," he joked, wiped the side of his face, and kissed her in the center of her head. "You smell like baby lotion," he told her.

When I spoke to his mother to inform her that I would be coming by, she asked whether they both could spend some time with Layla, and I agreed. I would come pick her up later during the week. I handed the baby bag over to Mrs. Travis. "She has about six outfits in there and a bunch of sleepers. Her bottle, formula, and cereal are inside. I feed her baby food too, so I put everything that you'll need inside for her," I said to Mrs. Travis. I suddenly got saddened because I would go days before seeing her again but Sayveon deserved to have a relationship and bond with her. She wasn't just my daughter; she was his too and I wanted to be fair.

"She's in good hands," Mrs. Travis promised.

Sayveon glanced up for a moment. "Dang, what's up, Stephanie. I ain't seen you in a long time."

"Hey. Yeah, I've been around."

I hugged my daughter and told her I loved her. Stephanie gave her goodbyes too. I handed Sayveon's keys to him, and we sneaked out before I witnessed Layla having a crying fit. I would call back and make sure she adjusted. Actually, it made me feel good to know that they would be bonding for a few days.

The Farm Life

Sparkle

The animals needed to be properly fed. It helped with their health and to ensure that they got the right supplements and vitamins to fatten them up to be later sold. We couldn't go another day without making sure that they were taken care of. I had gone out to the red barn with Ontavious a few times in the past so I had a good idea as to what to do. We grabbed a pair of rain boots from my closet and trampled down to the field. The huge cows, big bulls, and horses scared the hell out of me from the way that they stopped what they were doing and stared at us like we were from another planet.

"What the fuck are they looking at?" Steph asked and paused from walking.

"Girl, c'mon here. Let's get this over with." I proceeded to go on.

I kept going until I made it to the big barn. The cow and horse feed was inside of a small room right next to the wall along with a few shovels and other garden tools. We grabbed the big buckets on the floor, filled two of them with the corn feed, and carried the heavy containers over to two out of four feeding troughs. Stephanie and I went back the last time and filled up the others. The huge sized cows trotted over and began eating out of the long feeders. One looked to be the size of a baby elephant; it was so large. They all had different colors, and some had white patches in their faces. There was one in particular that I had seen

Ontavious pet several times when he would come over and see about them. I went over to the big black cow and rubbed her forehead before moving out of the way to let her go and eat.

"See, I told you it wouldn't be that bad," I said over my shoulder to Stephanie, but the look in her eyes told me she was spooked as hell. "Now, let's roll some hay out into the middle of the field so that they can eat off of that too."

"Dammit. I thought we were done. Let their fat asses eat the grass. That should be good enough." She huffed and puffed and stomped her foot. "You kno' I don't do animals. I'm tryna be nice, but I ain't wit' this shit right here."

"The grass is dying. Come on and stop acting a damn fool."

On one side of the barn, there was about fifty bales of hay. I rolled and pushed one big one, and she got the other until we made it to the center of the field. It was a hard job, but we did it. I gave Stephanie a high five. "You did good!"

"That wasn't as bad as I thought it would be," she said. As we went back toward the house, we joked about being turned into farmers.

"Oh, hell nah!" she let out. Not watching where she was going, she stepped in a huge pile of horseshit.

"You gotta look down while you're walking, girl."

"That's okay. I'll spray them down with the water hose and keep 'em outside for the next time I have to help you go out there."

"Let's go make some turkey sandwiches," I suggested.

"Okay, cool."

Suddenly we heard the thunder of pounding hooves and knew trouble was coming. We both turned around and picked up our pace when we saw what was heading our way. The reddish colored- bull was still a far ways back, so we gave it everything that we had and ran for our lives. Our legs churned wildly as we scurried, determined to get out of danger. The beating hooves were practically at our heels.

"Oh, we 'bout to be mauled by this big mothafucka!" Stephanie screamed with her hands flying in the air. She reached the gate and slung it open. We both made it through, and I slammed it shut behind me. I stopped and gasped for breath, but Stephanie continued running and hollering until she slipped down in a mud puddle right on her ass. Before I could go over and help her up, she leaped up like a jack-in-the-box and took off hopping and hollering with a brown mud stain on the back of her pants.

The bull stood with his dominating appearance and breathed heavily with his thick bones, large feet, muscular neck, large bony head, and ridges over the bloodshot red eyes. Short hair covered his body, but on the neck, and head he had curlier, wooly hair. The thick horns curved outwards in a flat arc. He used his horns to hit the fence and paced back and forth. That's what I called being bullied. There was no way in hell that I would ever try that again.

'Bout To Buck

Sayveon

Friday night had come and my fam Menace was about ten minutes away from Crystal Springs. I enjoyed every minute with my daughter, and Janay would be spending the whole weekend with us too. The older she got the more she looked like Peachy. I wanted Janay to do better than Peachy though and not be some bustdown, fuckin' a bunch of niggas.

The girls were in the bedroom wit' me playing wit' one another. Layla sat on Janay's lap playing with her nose and smiling. Her wide kool-aid smile reminded me so much of Sparkle. I had two gorgeous babies and vowed that only death would stop me from protecting them.

Janay looked at me. "Where's Sparkle?"

"I think she's at home. She's not my girlfriend right now."

"Well, who is your girlfriend now?" she asked. My shawdy's mind was always older than she was.

I cocked my head to the side 'cause she was somethin' else. "None of yo' business," I played.

"I got a boyfriend at school. His name is Merrion and when we get big we gonna-"

I cut her off midsentence, grabbed her face, and made her look at me. "Don't ever let me hear you talkin' 'bout a li'l boy. That shit ain't cool, and you need to have your head in a book not on a boy. Learn yo' ABC's and how to count to one hunnid," I scolded.

She poked her lip out. "I already know my ABC's, and I can count to twenty."

"Let me hear you say them then."

She began singing the ABC's song and then counted for me. I gave her a hug; and then, the doorbell rang. I heard Mama talking, so I got up with Layla in my arm and moved up front. "I'll be right back," I told Janay.

Menace and two other cousins of mine were in the living room. "I haven't seen my nephews in so long," Mama said as she hugged all three of 'em. "My goodness. Y'all smell like nothing but marijuana smoke. Y'all kno' better." She shook her head. "I kno' I ain't always been a Christian. I done it a long time ago, and that mess doesn't smell like what we smoked, that's strong."

They smiled. "Auntie you don't kno' 'bout that skunk smoke," Menace joked.

"If it smells like a skunk, I'm sure I wouldn't want to kno'."

When Menace spotted me, he gave me a gangsta hug and the proper handshake. His brothers came over and did the same. I hadn't seen his li'l brothers since our grandfather's funeral last year. Menace's mother and Mama were sisters so we were first cousins. Menace and I had always been close since we were young and I would go and stay with them in Memphis during the summer. We got into a lot of shit back then, and even back then, he was thugged out and didn't give a damn 'bout ridin' for his people. He lived by two words: love and loyalty.

Vicious and Bone were both two Youngblood's and 'bout that life. At twenty-three years old, Vicious stood about 5'9, medium built with smooth dark skin, and was all about his business. He was calm natured most of the time but the type niggas didn't wanna see heated. He kept his finger on the trigger. A blinged out gold and diamond chain hung down his neck with a Rolly on his wrist. Li'l cuz was clad in a fresh red t-shirt, black Levi's, and black and red J's on his feet. I could tell that he had been grinding and bubbled up in the game. I remembered when he and Vicious walked around the house wit' snotty noses and stayed gettin' their bad asses whooped by Aunt Norma back in the days.

Bone, on the other hand, happened to be the more talkative one and more outgoing. At nineteen he loved to be seen and stayed profiling with a dymed up piece of eye candy on his arm. Bone was tall, maybe 6'2 or 6'3, dark complexioned, and had dreads down his back wit' red tips right on the end. He kept his act-right on his waistline and had a sense of humor. He dressed in a red Adidas hoodie, dark blue jeans that sagged a li'l, and red and black Adidas on his feet. The iced-out piece in his ear had to be at least three-carats, and his arm was blinged out too. It was good to see the fam.

"This li'l girl is too cute to be yours," Menace jokingly said to me.

"She got all her looks from me." He reached out for Layla, but she turned her head. "She's trained not to go to ugly niggas," I kidded back. I called for Janay and she came up front and got introduced too.

"Where y'all gonna stay while y'all here?" Mama asked.

"We gon' find a hotel 'round here somewhere," Menace answered.

"No you won't. You all can stay right here until you get ready to go. Y'all kno' that my house is always open for family. Go back in there and get one of those three empty rooms and get comfortable," she said.

Over the years, she and her husband had turned the once only three bedrooms home into a bigger one. She loved her house and being outside in her rose garden. She took pride in her home and would open up for anyone that was family. She had a good heart and stayed in the kitchen cooking that good ole' soul food. That's what I loved about her. After my cousins finished taking their luggage in the bedrooms, Mama offered them something to eat. We all ate and then smashed out. As we rode, we discussed our next move.

Never A Dull Moment

Sparkle

Stephanie and I chilled in the house for the remainder of the week. Layla wouldn't be home for a few more days, and I hadn't gone out in forever. For some strange reason, I wanted to go out and have myself a good time. We were on the sofa watching a DVD of the old TV show 'Good Times' when I began to nod off to sleep from boredom.

"I'm bored as hell. Layla's gone, and I wanna go out somewhere. Let's get out and see what's goin' on in Jack-town," I said. I didn't hear Stephanie say anything back, so I looked over at her. She was sound asleep with one of her legs cocked up on the armrest. "Ay, wake up, hell!" I raised my voice louder. She jumped out of her sleep.

"Fuck you talkin' loud like that for?" She stretched her arms and sat up straight.

"I said that I wanna go out somewhere tonight. Let's hop up and put some clothes on. I need to be trying to take advantage of the baby not being here."

"I'm so sleepy that I don't kno' what to do," she said in a groggy and sleepy way.

I tossed a decorative pillow from the sofa at her and hit her on the head. "A'ight. Give me a few seconds to get up and start moving around. I'ma call Tank and tell him where we gon' be. I wanna kick it with him some. I'm kinda feeling him."

I brushed her off. "Whatever. I'm headed to go and start getting ready."

I took a hot shower. When I was done, I wrapped a big pink towel around me and walked over to the walk-in closet to choose an outfit. I found some gear that was classy but sexy and a pair of cute shoes to match. The short gold mini-dress that draped down to my waist in the back was perfect. I slid my foot in the six-inch matching gold stilettos. I put a gold and diamond tennis bracelet on my arm, gold earrings in my ears, and then stepped back to look at myself in the mirror. I knew that I looked the part, and nobody could tell me that I wasn't the shit. Leaning over in the sink, I rinsed my face with warm water, patted it dry, and used a light moisturizer. I used the eye brush to lightly apply bronzer to the eyelids, applied mascara, and finished my look off with a shiny coat of lip-gloss. I popped my lips for extra effect.

I used the flat irons to straighten my jet-black hair that flowed pass my shoulders. Once my hair was done I grabbed a gold handbag from the closet and gave myself another look in the mirror before walking out of the room. I yelled at Stephanie that I was ready and then sat in the living room area and waited for her.

After about an hour, big sis swayed in the room showing out in a short, fitted black dress, and leopard print mid-calf red bottom boots. She sported a cute pin up hairstyle with a bang. She swirled around in a circle. "I'm bad, huh?"

"You a'ight," I kidded.

"Undercover hater," she played back.

On our way to Jackson, I cracked the windows as I drove. It was a muggy night and the temperature had dropped down in the upper sixties, but this was the norm for Mississippi in October. Stephanie's cell phone rang. She answered and put it on speaker. It was Tank.

"What's up, stranger?" he said. The sound of loud rap music played in the background and we could hear people talking loud. It sounded like they were having a good time.

"How you been doing, Mister?" she asked him in a low tone trying to sound all sexy.

"Good. Ay, you and yo' sister should come through. Buck's having his birthday party tonight, and it's bangin' over here. It's at his crib, and we just parlaying and sitting back sippin' on some drinks and listening to good music."

"Okay. We will be there shortly to see what's goin' down over there."

"A'ight. Let me kno' when you're here, and I'll come outside." He then gave her the address, which was in Brandon, Mississippi.

"Okay I will call you," she said and hung up the phone.

She placed the phone in her lap and looked at me.

"You down?" Stephanie asked.

"Yeah, I'll go. It's not like I'm doin' shit else."

She typed the address into her phone's GPS, and it guided us. I had a feeling that we would have some fun, but if not, I sure knew my way back home.

We weaved in and out of the Friday night traffic in Jackson until we made it to the city of Brandon. We drove up to a stunning two-story mansion overlooking the Barnett Reservoir. Outside security held flashlights and directed the cars to park on the huge spacious yard side by side in a line. We sat and waited bumper to bumper to go in. All kinds of fly foreign whips rolled through. We waited maybe ten more minutes before making it up to the house. I parked right beside a new-modeled sparkling white Cadillac Escalade truck on a set of chrome wheels.

Stephanie hit up Tank, and he said he'd come right out. We both got out and pranced up to the crib. I was in the world of ballers and looked as fierce as the broads surrounding me. Being a dyme piece required doing more than wearing fly gear. It's all about the attitude. Just being honest, I was on it and felt that Steph and I were the baddest broads there.

Tank swaggered out and stepped to us. "Y'all follow behind me," he told us both. "They wit' me," he said to the bodyguards that stood right at the door checking off on the invitation list making sure nobody got in that wasn't invited. I felt like I had been invited to a celebrity event when we got in. It was packed from wall to wall with ballers draped in jewels and encircled by hoes. The sound of 2Chainz featuring Drake, 'No Lie' could be heard throughout. The place was phenomenal. It was loaded with wide antique doors, solid wood floors, lead glass windows, twelve-foot ceilings, and unbelievable moldings. The decked out home wasn't the only thing that caught my attention. Guests chose food from a super big buffet and ate while standing up communicating with one another. About five topless gold- body painted cocktail waitresses pranced by the invited visitors in high heeled gold red bottom shoes holding platters with drinks on top.

From a distance, I could see a few well-known rappers conversing with others and mingling while drinking from wine glasses. The floor was full of women dancing and poppin' their asses to the beat of the song. David Banner stood near a wall with a few people talking. Jeezy strolled through with his soldiers on his heels. I'm a loyal fan, but I held my composure and didn't act thirsty.

Buck came out of nowhere, grabbed my hand with his left hand and held a bottle of Dom Perignon in the other. I left Stephanie and Tank behind as he led me to the backyard area. Outside there were large palm trees, a water frontage with a concrete sea wall, a striking granite pool, and a covered double boat slip. It had a tropical feel and lots of seating areas, but most of them were full of women sitting in their half naked outfits and dudes gawking. Some joined in on the fun and jumped in the water. He invited me to take a seat in an unoccupied area where I could hear the torrents of water gushing into the reservoir. It sounded soothing to the soul.

My body seemed to be drawn to him, like a bee to honey. I took in his confident attitude, ruggedly handsome appearance, and his 6'2 built body. He had a smooth swagger, dark chocolate skin, along with a self-assured personality. Fitted in a black short-sleeved logo Louis Vuitton t-shirt and LV initial belt, black Levi jeans, and a fresh pair of Vuitton high top sneakers, his character matched his clothing style. He had his gear game up and on point. I was diggin' him and although he was the definition of thugged out, I could tell that he wasn't the average street dude. He had tattoos all over his body and neck, iced out diamond stud earrings in both ears, gold chains around his neck, and he talked in a slang so deep it would qualify as its own language.

"I didn't kno' that you knew some rappers. You didn't tell me that you were doin' it like that," I said, breaking the ice.

"If you're real than you don't have to brag or boast about who you kno' or mention your money. Your wealth is understood. I have sick connections that I never bring up because er'body already kno's that I hang wit' the right people." He took a few swallows from the bottle. "Name droppin' shows a lack of confidence. I'm cool wit' myself; I don't need to let the people I hang wit' up my status."

"I agree."

"I'm feeling your vibe. I've been thinkin' about you since we met at the club. I didn't press you for your number because you told me that you were involved with someone. I had to respect it." Buck made eye contact when he talked.

"I was then, but we aren't together anymore."

"Program my number and hit me up sometimes so we can go out and get to know each other a li'l better." He called out his phone number, and I stored it in my cell.

"I love the sound of the water. It's relaxing and helps me to forget about my problems."

"I come out here all the time when I need a piece of mind. Sometimes I need to get away from everything and everybody. Feel me?"

"I do. I get like that too. So, do you have any kids? I forgot to ask you that the last time I talked to you," I snooped, poking my nose in his business.

"Damn, I must look like I got some kids somewhere?" He smiled and said, "A set of twin boys. What about you?"

"I have one daughter. She's seven months."

"You got a li'l baby. My boys are thirteen and think they grown, but they ain't. They remind me of how I was at that age."

I felt privileged that out of all of the ladies inside he chose to spend some time with only me. There were nice looking women everywhere flirting and being attention whores. I must have stood out from the rest.

"This is a new generation. These kids aren't how we used to be. They come out of the womb thinking that they know everything and can't nobody tell them nothing."

Suddenly a woman who I had seen around somewhere rudely interrupted our conversation. I just couldn't place her at the time. She flounced up in a see through off-the-shoulder black top that exposed her black bra and tight fitted short skirt. Her long weave flowed down her back and stopped at her butt. My eyes moved from her outfit down to her black peep-toe pumps. The broad moved her hair out of her face and tapped her foot on the ground.

"Excuse me, but you aren't entertaining your company, Birthday Boy," she slowly said to him. She held a cup halfway full of liquor in her hand and a cigarette in the other. She reached over in her bra and came out of it with a lighter. She clicked the lighter until it flamed but she tried to light the wrong end of it. Her movements told me that the alcohol had her twisted.

"I'm coming back in. I'm sittin' back chillin' right now."

"Anyway, how you been doing? I haven't heard from you in a while."

"I'm straight. What's been up wit' you?"

"Making my money and doin' me," she stated. She looked me up and down and then I remembered who the chick was.

I frowned and under my breath went, "Ugh."

"What the fuck you tryna say, bitch?" she asked me.

I got up in her grill. We were almost nose-to-nose. "It don't matter what I just said, hoe. You ain't gonna do a damn thing about it. You better stay in your lane and speak when your dick lips are spoken to." I figured that things were about to go sour because LaShune who happened to be Nakia's sister held a grudge against me for cutting up Nakia.

LaShune pushed me in the chest. "You better back the fuck up."

That's when I let her have it and tapped that jaw with a quick right hook. She didn't back down. Matter of fact, she punched right back. I caught a handful of the long weave and off came her lace front wig. Her eyes grew big as two soccer balls and she retaliated by clawing, punching, and pulling my hair. Buck got between us and begged LaShune to let go of my hair. I continued to swing off on her popping her all upside the head. Finally, she let go.

I charged into her knocking her down to the ground. I put my hands around her throat and started choking her out. When I thought that she had had enough of that and was on the verge of passing out, I clocked her with a mean blow to the face. Somehow, she used all of the power that she had to flip me off her. We rolled repeatedly passing licks and name-calling until we both landed in the pool. With my hair wet and outfit stuck to me from the water, I never stopped banging that skull in. I used my hands to push her head under. She squirmed and kicked for me to stop, but I didn't until a few dudes who were already in there pulled us away from each other.

People swarmed around and watched us throw down. A few of them held up their phones, videotaping the bullshit. I wouldn't have been the least bit surprised if I ended up on You Tube.

When I got out of the water, Buck said to me, "Babygirl, you gonna have to watch that temper. Yo' clothes fucked up now. I mean, I kno' that ole girl can talk a bunch of shit, but you shoulda ignored her."

"I ain't goin'."

"I understand all that, but this ain't the place for that bullshit."

"Well you kno' what? Fuck your place. I don't have to be here. I'm leaving. I'm the wrong person for you to be checking. That gutter rat came over starting with me," I fired back.

He grabbed me by the arm. "Calm your ass down. First off, I like a woman who has respect for herself and I appreciate one that can hold her own. I'm not saying that you're wrong for defending yourself because I probably would have done the same thing, but you should have let me handle her."

"You ain't talking about nothing. I'm out." I tossed up the deuces and was leaving when out of nowhere LaShune hit me over the head with her shoe. I raised my hands, covered my face, and ended up pulling her to the ground. She fell down. I decked her in the face. She couldn't do shit but scream and yell. I grabbed her hair and snatched on it as hard as I could. By the time a man got me off her, I had jerked her hair out in certain spots and she had more patches than a quilt.

I was heading to find Stephanie so we could leave when she ran up to me. "Tank told me you were out here scrapping."

"I had to beat a hoe down, and I'm ready to go."

"World Starrr!" a baritone voiced male hollered out.

Ignoring it all, I kept it moving.

"Let me go and tell Tank that I'm leaving. I'll head to your ride as soon as I find him," Stephanie said and took off back inside.

Even though I was already leaving, LaShune and I were both escorted off the property by a big tall and dark bouncer. When we made it out front, he made sure LaShune got in her car first and drove off. Then he watched me get in my vehicle.

"Have a good night and drive careful," he said before walking away.

"Yeah, whatever," I mumbled.

A few minutes went by before Stephanie made it to the car. I was giving her the run down when my phone went off indicating that I had a message. I reached under my seat where I hid my handbag before going inside of the mansion. I handed my bag to Stephanie and told her to get my phone out and to read the message since I didn't want to text and drive. When she told what was on the screen, I tripped out.

'Nawlins'

Sayveon

Instead of kicking it at the same spots in the Sipp that night, we hit the slab headed for New Orleans. 'Nawlins' was the place to kick it. It was known for its food, jazz, and Mardi Gras festival that was held in the city. We ended up at a club called Bourbon Heat in the French Quarter. Menace drove one of his many rides. On that night, he pushed a new-modeled snowflake- white Range Rover Sport on a set of custom painted white and chrome '26 inch wheels. I rolled up behind him in the Benz, and we parked side by side. After murdering the engine, I stepped out of the car. Menace and my li'l cousins got out of his ride and walked over to me, and we all walked to wait in line to get inside.

Once inside I swaggered through the club blessing the crowd with my tatted up presence. The fit was all Ralph Lauren from my head down to the kicks on my feet. I sported a long sleeved dark denim button down shirt, long khaki pants, and leather brown Polo strap boots. My dreads hung down my back and I knew I had a good chance of pulling any hoe in there from the way they stared me down like hungry vultures. Any woman could tell that I was a moneymaking king from the way I looked and the Gucci Guilty cologne that I splashed on had me smelling like one too.

I could vibe with the place. It was a 3-in-1-bar with a second level. I moved around scoping out the scenery. The downstairs consisted of the front bar which had many types of liquor to choose from. In the back of the downstairs area, there was a large spacious patio with another small bar and restrooms. Being that it was a bit cool outside, they had heaters all over the patio. Upstairs had been divided into two parts. On one side there was a huge dance floor and a bar off to the side. A female DJ spinned the latest pop and hip-hop music. Half-naked hoes twerked on the dance floor. I wasn't the least bit interested in any of them and started to walk on when one in particular caught my eye. The Creole female had been cursed wit' gorgeousness. She had a fair skin complexion, soft, light-brown, long bouncy hair that stopped midways her back and a well-proportioned body. Her long legs stood her at about 5'8 in height, but maybe she looked taller because of her high-heeled shoes. Shawdy was a perfect ten.

The unknown young broad rocked a backless ocean-blue figure huggin' black cat suit. We made eye contact for a minute before she looked away and started back moving her body. I made a mental note to get at her before I left that night and moved along. I walked to the other side where there was a big balcony. People were sitting out watching the tourists and others down below.

"I see some bitches I'm 'bout to get at," Bone said as we went back in and over to the bar.

A white female wit' red hair, a large black nose ring and a pierced tongue was the bartender behind the counter. "Let me get a Hurricane," I told her after we all sat down on the barstools. She gave me a head nod in acknowledgement. Before she turned and walked away, all three of my cousins asked her to make them one too. We could see her mixing light and dark rum, passion fruit juice, orange and lime juice, syrup, and grenadine. She poured it all into a cocktail shaker, shook it, and strained it into three lamp-shaped glasses that she garnished with a cherry and lime slice. She brought the drinks over and placed all three in front of us. I had to have a Hurricane because the drink was invented there, and I knew they knew how to hook it up just right. Menace peeled off a c-note from the wad in his pocket and slid it across the table to her. The white girl got him some change and passed it to him.

I took several swallows from the drink and sat back watching the clubbers do their 'thang' on the dance floor. Ole' girl had me in a trance, the way she shook that phatty and dropped it. I couldn't help but wonder what that pussy was hittin' like. When the song went off she walked off the floor and leaned back against the wall, joining two of her home girls who had left the dance floor too. One of her girls was a short brown-skinned female, and the other was taller and honey complexioned. All were dyme pieces and from the way they dressed and carried themselves, I knew that they were used to being pampered. When the timing was right, I'd push up on it and put some boss game in her ear.

Rage

Sparkle

Stephanie had opened the attached message from Ontavious, and a pic of his big dick popped up on the screen. I screamed out, almost tickled to death. The things mothafuckas would do when they desperately wanted you back. After the pic, my cell rang. Stephanie told me it was Ontavious and handed me the phone. I answered without hesitation.

"Where are you?" Ontavious asked.

"Out minding my own damn business."

"I need to see you."

"Not tonight you won't, and honestly, I don't want to hear shit that you got to say."

I held the phone with one hand and wheeled into Arby's fast food restaurant with the other. I had gotten hungry as hell. I noticed that Stephanie was mighty quiet so I glanced over at her staring at her cell phone. I moved the phone away from my mouth. "Girl, what are you over there looking at that has you in a zone?"

"I forwarded that picture message to my phone from yours. This 'nicca' dick so big and long he can make a neck tie out of it," she joked in a low voice.

"Hold on," I said to Ontavious. I took her phone out of her hand to delete the photo when I saw that she had aligned two images side by side and made a collage.

"I was trying to see which one had the biggest pole. I think Tank might have him beat by an inch."

I gave her a look that said, "Girl please." I erased Ontavious' penis shot and the collage and told her, "You ain't nothing but a damn freak and for the record I think 'O' got Tank beat." I didn't get mad or even the least bit upset with her because I knew that Stephanie was a natural born fool.

"Are you there?" I heard him ask.

"I told you to hold on for a minute. I had to do something."

"I'm sorry. I didn't hear you."

The drive- thru line only had one car in front of me. I took a second glance at the vehicle to be sure that it was who I thought it was, and of course, it happened to be LaShune in her car. She sat at the menu screen for about two minutes before the employee spoke and asked if she could help her. I let my window down waiting for my turn to pull up. "Let me get the beef and cheddar sandwich, a small fry, and large lemonade." Her speech was still slurred from her being twisted off the alcohol from the party.

"Let me order my food, I'll holla back some other time," I told Ontavious and hung up before he could respond.

"Ain't that the girl you just got into a fight with?" Stephanie curiously asked.

"Yep."

The girl taking the order didn't say nothing for a minute and then came back on the speaker. "I'm sorry repeat your order for me again."

Offended and liquored-up, she repeated her order. Again, there was a brief silence before the worker came back. "Ma'am, I do apologize, but the fries haven't been dropped in the fryer yet. It'll be about seven minutes on them if you wanted to wait."

"Hell nah! I'll starve waiting on those bastards to get ready!" LaShune yelled out to the girl, "Fuck the fries just give me my drink and the sandwich." She was given her total, and then she pulled up to the first window and paid.

"She's so damn ghetto," I mumbled.

She drove to the second window, snatched the bag and drink from the person that handed it over and drove off.

"Thanks for stopping by Arby's how can I help you?" the young girl asked.

"Let me get the Arby's Melt and a large sweet tea," I said. Stephanie told me what she wanted, and I said, "Add a French Dip and Swiss sandwich and a bottled water."

"No problem. Drive up to the first window for your total."

I handed her a twenty-dollar bill, got the food and change, and we bailed. Thank goodness, she didn't give us a hard time. I reached into the bag, grabbed my food, and munched down on it before slowing down and stopping at a red light. I was sitting at the light when I noticed LaShune across the street at a gas station. She was finishing pumping gas. She put the top on the gas tank and pulled out of the parking lot into the lane right beside me.

She let her window down and hollered out of it, "Get out and get another ass whooping, stank bitch!"

"Girl, boo. Sit your funky ass down somewhere!" I roared. I overlooked her because I knew that she was smashed and I was tired and ready to go on to the house. I had a long drive and wasn't in the mood to be tongue battling with a drunk. I sped off down the street. When I got to another traffic light, I slowed down because it was turning red. I felt a hard hit and looked in the rearview. LaShune had rammed into the back of my SUV with her vehicle.

"You kno' what? You gonna have to put them 'thangs' on her head again because she's going too far with this shit!" Stephanie said.

I got out and examined my bumper, which didn't have a scratch or dent. I was lucky because I thought for sure that she had done some damage. "Get yo' punk ass up out of there!" I stood there and waited for her to make a move so that we could lock up.

LaShune didn't get out, instead she sped off. I hopped in my vehicle and got right behind her. I got right on her tail. Stephanie rolled her window down, but I didn't know what she intended to do. She grabbed a small silver and black .25 from her purse and aimed it at the sky. Pow! Pow! Pow! LaShune's vehicle swayed from side to side before crashing into a power pole. I panicked and got ghost. The whole way home, I wondered if LaShune was dead or alive.

The Wrong Shit

Sayveon

Ole girl that I had been peepin' out eventually came over to the bar and ordered a Pomegranate Margarita. She bounced down in an empty seat beside me.

"I haven't seen you here before. Is this your first time coming?" she asked.

"Yeah."

"How do you like it so far?"

"It's a'ight. I'm just sitting back coolin' and having a good drink." I switched topics. "What's your name babygirl?"

"Lanelle."

"That's what's up. I'm Sayveon."

"I like that name. It's very different."

"That's because I'm a different type of nigga. I ain't average," I bragged.

"I see that you aren't."

As we were making small talk, I remembered that I had left my phone out in the car on the charger. I excused myself from the bar and walked toward the door. When I got to the door, I asked security if it were okay for me to grab my cell from my whip After he okayed it, I went to the Benz and retrieved it. I checked my phone for any missed calls or text messages and noticed that I had a picture message that was sent an hour earlier from someone I hadn't expected to hear from. It had been a while since I had held a conversation wit' her. I opened the message and there was a picture of Sparkle cupcakin' with some nigga as they sat down somewhere. It was from LaShune. I text her back, Fuck you sending this shit to me for?

I turned to go back in the club when my cell rang. LaShune's number popped up on the screen. I didn't answer because I didn't want to hear that shit about what Sparkle was out there doing. I was heated, but there wasn't nothin' that I could do from Louisiana. I wasn't tryna fuck up my night 'bout that right there. I was at that club to get fucked up and chill in a relaxed mode. I'd handle all that other shit when I got back to Mississippi. I went on back in to go mack on Lanelle and get between those thick thighs.

***

I spit game on shawdy, and she agreed to let me come hang out at her crib. I told my cuzzos that I'd catch up wit' them the following morning and dipped out of the place. I followed behind her white Nissan Sentra until we ended up at her pad. She opened up the door to her house and let me inside. The living room was a bit small, but it was neat and organized. She had a black leather sofa and a glass coffee table with the matching end tables. There was a nice sized flat screen television on the wall. It was on, but neither one of us paid it any attention because the liquor in our systems had us both feelin' freaky as fuck. She told me to have a seat and then said, "Take your pants off. Lemme see that dick."

"You might not be ready for this right here," I said and grabbed my crotch. My dick was hard, so the length and thickness could be seen from the way I held on to it. I unbuttoned and then unzipped my pants and took them off along with the boxers. Our eyes locked together. Our heads slowly met, and she bit down on my bottom lip. Our tongues locked and moved in and out of each other's mouths.

I lifted my shirt over my head and tossed it to the floor leaving me butt ass naked. I bent over and grabbed a rubber from my pants pocket. Shid, I didn't know this bitch. I strapped up, and before she could move, I grabbed her by the legs and pulled her nearly off the couch. I pulled off her panties and lifted one leg in the air. I pushed down into the pussy and went knee deep ramming in her. I stared deep into her eyes and thought about how good the shit felt, but all of that went flat-line when an odor ran up my nose. What the fuck? I kno' damn well this hoe ain't smelling like hot garbage. My dick gon' melt off in this hot nasty shit. I snatched out and stood back up. "Man, yo' pussy stank," I said to her and fanned my nose. The whole room smelled like a goddamn fish market in the middle of summer.

She bucked her eyes from embarrassment and then got slick. "Nigga please, you got to be smelling your musty nuts."

"Find whatever died in yo' pussy and pull that shit out, bitch," I snapped back.

I hurried and put my boxers and pants on. I grabbed my shirt as I ran out of the door. I had to get up out of there, fast. I remembered somethin' Sparkle had said to me a long time ago. "Nigga, you gonna keep on until you run up on some shit that you don't want." She was right and everything that looks good damn sho' ain't.

Calming Down From It All

Sparkle

The only sound that could be heard from where I laid was the sound of crickets. The room was dark as I closed my heavy eyelids thinking about what had just happened. No lie, it scared me almost to death. It seemed as though my life had spiraled out of control and things had gone from bad to worse. True enough, I didn't like LaShune or her sister, but I didn't want anyone to lose their life on my behalf. I wished she had of just left me the hell alone and none of that bullshit would have taken place. But nooo she had to keep fuckin' with me like I'm some Toys R' Us kid that needed to be played with. I shoved all thoughts of what had gone on to the back of my mind, and after tossing and turning, I finally drifted off to sleep.

I hadn't been asleep long before I heard loud knocks coming from the front door. Whoever it was, they were beating so hard that it sounded like the door would collapse. My heart began to race because I had already been on paranoid about the car accident earlier. I got out of the bed, put on house shoes, and raced up front.

"Oh my God," I mumbled, growing angry because my sleep had been interrupted.

I peered out of the blinds, huffed, twisted the doorknob and opened the door. "I needed to see you, and where the hell have you been all night? I've come up here twice, and both times I saw that you were gone," Ontavious stated.

"It's almost two o'clock in the morning. I don't need you coming here askin' me questions like you're still my man. Go find that hoe you been havin' at your house and talk to her. I ain't got no talk for you. It's just that simple."

"Well, just let me come in," he pleaded.

"I don't want to be bothered."

"Let me in and just give me a few minutes of your time."

I gave in and let him come inside and have a seat. I turned on a lamp and patiently waited for him to say whatever it was that he needed to get off of his chest so that I could go back and sleep.

"There's nothing that I can say that can repair the damage that I've done to our relationship. I now recognize that. I made a mistake and had a lapse in judgment. I want you to know how sorry I am, and it gnaws at me to know that I hurt you so badly. I shouldn't have been associating with another woman, and there is no excuse for that. I should have worked harder to communicate with you before assuming that you were trying to get back with your ex."

"I can't be with someone who doesn't trust me. Then, you retaliated by bringing another woman to church with you. That's unforgivable."

"Can you find it somewhere in your heart to forgive me and give me another chance?" he asked.

I had been thinking things over. I did care and love Ontavious, but what he did hurt me to my heart and made me feel like he was taking me back through the same shit that Sayveon had put me through. I had promised myself that I'd never let another man make me feel less than a woman by cheating on me, but the good outweighed the bad and I loved the person that he was. Besides, I wasn't perfect myself, and we all make mistakes every now and then. I would forgive him, but I damn sure wouldn't be forgetting anything.

I pointed my finger at him to show how serious I was while saying, "I'm not going to let up on you. You're going to have to show and prove that I'm who you want."

"I will. I regret pulling away from you physically and emotionally." He held my hand in his. "I don't want to lose you, and I don't want to hurt you this way ever again. I know this can't be fixed with just a plain old apology, but I offer it anyway because I need you to know how apologetic I am and how much I still love you. Please don't give up on me."

The words that came from his mouth lay heavy on my heart, and I could feel the pain in his voice with each word that he spoke. "I love you too, baby," I whispered with my voice cracking from the emotions that ran through my body.

He still held on to my hand but rubbed the side of my face with his other. "I wish I could take all of this back, but I can't. All I can do is show you how much I regret what I've done. We've had a few minor problems in the past, but we've always been able to work through them. I think we're stronger because of them, and this situation is no different. I will do whatever it takes for you to trust me again, so things can get back to the way they were. We've had too many good times to break up over this. Can we make-up?"

We had a stare down; I felt myself getting turned on by his gray eyes and handsome face. My kitty slowly began to feel wet and slippery. I looked down at the seat of his pants, and his budge had begun to rise. No wonder I loved him so much; he's not only pleasing to the eye but also is blessed with a nice sized bedroom-pleaser.

"You looking like you've never seen what I'm packing before." Ontavious laughed, rubbing his hand up and down his big and long piece of meat.

He slowly licked his lips. "Let's do the nasty."

I smiled at his request and raised my brow as I chuckled a tad bit. My heart began beating fast as my eyes wondered all over his body. He slid over to me and brought his lips close to my neck, kissing me softly as he pulled my teddy up over my head. His mouth up against my skin had me throbbing, my body temperature was getting higher and higher.

"Stand up, baby," he whispered in my ear.

I stood, and he leveled his body with my hips. His hands caressed me up my legs, and he eased my thong to the floor. I stood there as naked as the day I entered the world. I could feel his warm touch sliding between my legs, his palm grazing against my thigh. The closer he got to my sensitive spot, the hotter I got. Ontavious used the tip of his fingers to tickle my clit. I let out a soft moan, bit down on my bottom lip, and spread my legs a little wider.

"Spread 'em out more, baby," he instructed. I did as I was told. He let out a deep breath, cupped my ass, and buried his face right in my pussy. I placed my hand on top of his head and looked down at him slurping and moving his tongue in and out of my juicy wet hole. He tilted his head to the side and wiggled his moist and warm tongue up and down my wetness. "You gonna cum for me?" he wanted to know. I shoved his head back where it belonged and he licked even faster than before.

A low, "Ummm," came out, and I could feel the orgasm coming on strong, fluttering through my veins. Not being able to hold back anymore, I let go of the best feeling that I had felt in a long time. Ontavious' mouth was covered in my juice.

"Sparkle, is everything okay?" Stephanie hollered from her room.

I hurried and put my nightie back on. "I'm straight. Me and Ontavious are talking."

"A'ight," she yelled back.

It wasn't over between me and Ontavious just yet. I led him into the bedroom and told him to undress for me. He took off everything, then picked me up and placed me on the bed. He fucked me senseless in every position, digging every inch of himself in and out of me. My coochie sizzled, and I almost bust off again. He removed my legs from his shoulders and fell back on the bed. It was my turn to take over.

I brought myself over him and spread in a Chinese slit, both of my legs straight out against the bed. My palms were flat on his chest as I used all my upper body strength to bounce on his joint.

"Look at you." Ontavious groaned, planting his hands on my round phatty.

"Shh." I giggled with a soft moan, feeling every inch of him enter me.

I stared down at his face as I brought myself down on him hard. My coochie was so wet that I could hear the squishy sounds as I came down on him; his stomach was even soaked with my liquid.

"Damn baby, I'ma cum," he moaned, pushing his hips against mine.

That didn't stop me. I lifted myself up and down, down and up, and his rock hard stick got harder inside of me with each pump. I moaned loudly as I felt my body beginning to shake. Bringing myself up one more time, I slammed down on him and at the same time, we came, our moans filling the room.

He held me down on him as his long pole twitched inside of me. The way his dick throbbed against my pussy walls drove me insane. He was so deep. I felt so good as the orgasm released from my body.

I let myself collapse on top of Ontavious and pressed my head against his chest. I could hear his heart pounding away as I laid there catching my breath. He breathed against my hair as he caressed me up and down my back. After a while, I rolled off him and rested in his arms. I didn't know that I had missed him as much as I had. Our sex session was exactly what I needed, and he delivered right on time. I fell off to sleep with the man that I truly loved laying right beside me.

Treacherous Mothafuckas

Sayveon

My cousins and I all had rooms next to each other at The Bourbon Orleans Hotel in The French Quarter. Menace, Vicious, and Bone had gotten up wit' some broads from the club and were posted up wit' 'em. I went in and decided to take a hot bath to ease my mind, tryin' not to think about Lanelle and how she fucked up my whole night smellin' like a fresh can of tuna. I had plans on knockin' that pussy out but had to dip on her.

I felt like I needed a nice hot bath, so I filled the large Jacuzzi style tub with hot water. Once the tub was full, I got out of all of my clothes and got in. I had the water as hot as I could stand it. I blocked out er'thang and rested my head on the back of the wall, relaxing. The sound of my cell disturbed me, and I wondered who could have been dialing me at that time of the morning. I remembered that I had left it on the bed and decided I wasn't gettin' out of the tub to go and answer it. I let the phone ring as I closed my eyes, and my thoughts soon fell on Sparkle and Layla. I had never seen Sparkle wit' another dude before, and just bein' real, it bothered me. I'm real and would show er'thang but signs of weakness, but looking at that pic that LaShune sent hurt me and rested heavy on my chest. I re-blocked the image from my head.

I pictured a life wit' Sparkle and wondered if I could do right by her. Yeah, it wounded me a li'l to kno' that another nigga was gettin' her time and attention, but she would always have a special place in my heart. I'd sit back and let her do her. If this is what she wanted, she'd come back to me and we'd make it work. Until then, I would have fun living the life of a bachelor and making myself happy.

I realized I had been soaking for about thirty minutes, and I snapped out of my zone. I washed my body wit' a small white towel, grabbed a big towel and dried off, and got out of the tub. I grabbed a white wife beater from my luggage and a pair of black boxers and got dressed. I checked my cell and saw it was LaShune and decided to call her back.

"Hello," she answered wit' an attitude.

"Fuck you want?" I asked, frowns had begun to cover my forehead cause she was aggravating the shit out of me.

"I need to know why my sister has been contacting you?" Oh, goddamn. I recognized the sound of the voice right then. It wasn't LaShune calling it was Nakia.

"Ask your sister. I ain't got no talk fo' you."

She huffed and puffed and said, "I would ask her but-" I didn't let her finish explaining what she had to say because I gave that hoe the dial tone. She called back, but I didn't answer. I didn't feed into the bullshit she was trying to start up. My phone started ringing again. When I looked at the screen I didn't recognize the number, so I picked up.

"Sup?" I asked the caller.

"See, that's why I fucked your boy, and to keep from wasting your time and mine too, let me tell you this- This is Rich's baby, and I will take care of mine on my own. I got this. And while you were running around here fucking any trick ass bitch that crossed your path, I was getting piped down by your friend. I told LaShune that this wasn't your baby, and now I know exactly why you were screaming that you wanted a blood test."

"When you get through talkin' all that fuck shit, I still won't give a damn. I ain't gon' miss one minute of sleep because you got fucked by Rich. I ain't mad at you cause a hoe, gonna be a hoe and I can't change that."

"Don't call me out of my name, mothafucka!"

"I'm a certified nigga, and I kno' that y'all chickens only try to fuck wit' me 'cause I got figures. That's one reason that I never try to save y'all bitches. I just bust a nut and move on. So, you ain't sayin' shit."

"LaShune's wrong, and you are too but-"

I didn't let her finish what she had to say. I pressed end on the phone screen and the words, CALL ENDED popped up. I put both numbers on spam and call block; I wasn't tryna get wit' LaShune or Nakia like that no more. It was a wrap wit' those two. All of my old females true colors had come out. They were unloyal and couldn't be trusted. I would have to find a whole new stable of thoroughbred bitches.

And Another One

Sayveon

I sat on the side of the bed with my foot cocked up watching the throwback movie, Menace To Society. When I heard a few taps coming from the door, I got up and asked who it was.

"It's me, Cuz, this Bone."

I let him in. "Damn, nigga ain't you supposed to be over there hittin' that?" I teased.

"You kno' me, bruh. I already did that. Check this, the one I'm with say she got a homegirl that wanna come and hook up with you. What's poppin', you down with that shit?"

"I'm straight." After dealin' wit' the last bitch, I wasn't even in the mood for fuckin' wit' no hoes that way.

He laughed. "I asked ole' girl to tell her to make sure she washes that ass before she comes," he joked after I gave him the story on the last hoe.

I chuckled. "A'ight, give her my number, and I'll check her out."

"Man, we came down here to get right, and fuck somethin'. All these fine broads roaming around this state, shit you better cop one of 'em. All of 'em ain't got skunk pussy."

"Bet that," I said and he walked out.

I waited for her to give me a ring and when she did, we chopped it up for about ten minutes before she agreed to meet me so we could hang out for a while.

***

I walked out of the room when Shaneeka tol' me she was down there in the lobby waiting for me. I didn't get my hopes up high because normally when I did and went on blind dates, the female was busted up in the face and didn't look worth shit. I caught the elevator down to the first floor. From how she described herself on the phone, I knew it was her looking out of the glass in the elevator. Shawdy was lookin' tight in a short auburn brown skirt, long sleeved fitted black shirt that hung off the shoulder, and black spiked heels. Her caramel brown legs looked nice and smooth, and I knew she was flawless.

As I neared her, I called out her name. "Shaneeka."

She turned around and said, "What's up? Are you Sayveon?"

I deepened my voice. "Nah, I'm his cousin from Mississippi. He said he's sorry for the inconvenience and er'thang, but he's upstairs throwing up and shittin' er'where. You might catch that shit. It'll be best if you go on back home."

She smiled, showing off her gold that went straight across her top grill wit' the word B-O-S-S-Y embedded. I couldn't go out like that though. Her mouth took up like half her face, nose was wider than a church door, full lips, and she had a biggo forehead. I stepped back 'cause lookin' at her made me wanna take off running.

"Well what's yo' name, 'bebae'?" She pronounced baby wit' her deep accent.

"Antonio," I lied.

"Can I go back up with you?"

"I'm married," I made up.

I turned and began to walk away. As I was headed back to the elevator, I noticed the front desk clerk. She was on the phone taking a call. She looked up at me, flashed me a blushing smile, and then dropped her head back down. I went back to my room with a new agenda.

Gotta Go

Stephanie

After getting the call that I had waited a long time for, I told Tank that I would meet him somewhere, and he arranged for us to meet up in Canton. Canton wasn't that far from where I was in Camden. The liquor had us both feeling a li'l horny, and I needed him to put my fire out. I couldn't take it anymore. I tossed on a pair of dark colored jeans, a white baby tee, sneakers, and a light jacket then I went and hollered at Sparkle. "Sparkle, let me use your Infiniti. I need to go somewhere. I'll take care of it."

From her groggy tone, I knew that I had woke her up. "Where the hell do you call yourself going this time of the morning, girl?"

"I'm going to meet Tank."

I could hear her feet hit the floor. She came out of her room with an attitude. "No. You need to get Aunt Ruby's car and go on. I forgot to put gas in mine and plus I'm going to go and get my oil changed later on."

"You kno' that car is a piece of shit."

"Girl, please."

She twirled and went back into her room. I had no other choice but to drive the hoopmobile. Which would be embarrassing as hell, but I didn't have any more options. I got the keys to the car, locked up, and went outside. I remembered I had to get in on the passenger side and slide over to the driver's seat. I put the key in the ignition and turned it. It tried to start but then shut down. I patted the gas about three times and re-tried it again. The next time it started right on up, and I took off to meet Tank.

I had a nice ride without any complications out of the old vehicle. I parked right beside Tank, got out, and greeted him. "Hey, baby."

"You good?" he asked.

"I'm aight. I had to drive this old thing because my sister wouldn't let me get her ride."

"That's okay," he said with a smile. "Follow me."

The Hampton Inn was a nice hotel. We stopped at the front first. Tank paid, got the key, and we went up. When we got in there, I sat down on the clean and comfortable bed. I surveyed the room and there was a flat screen T.V., microwave, and fridge and everything looked good. Thinking back over my life, I had seen some of the most run down and disgusting roach motels. Compared to where I had laid my head down in the past, this was considered spick and span. Those days were now over, and I didn't intend to go back. I forgot all about the history of me being on drugs when Tank started giving four-play. He eventually put on a condom. I was down for whatever.

Before long, our clothes were on the floor, and we both had gotten in the bed. There wasn't an inch of me that his mouth didn't explore- from the base of my throat, to the curve of my waist, to the back of my knees down to my ruby-red toenails. When he went down and tasted the already damp petals of my womanhood, I gripped the sheets and arched my hips as the tremors of ecstasy shook my body. I knew that he felt each intense spasm as if I was connected to him.

Our bodies moved as one as we both rocked and stirred from the feeling that swept through us. With the last bit of self-control, he held on until he couldn't take it any longer. Then he plunged deep and buried his face in my neck.

"Goddamn," he groaned over and over as the lightning bolts of fulfillment shot through him. We clung together after the rush of sensation that was shared between us both. We lay in a state of complete exhaustion. Tank moved first and rolled off me. He propped himself on one elbow and gazed down at me.

"You're so beautiful," he said, still breathing irregularly.

"You think so?" I blushed.

"Oh, yeah." He nodded his head. This man had my mind so blown. I was falling for him, already.

Saturday Morning Sunshine

Sayveon

Early that morning I had a visitor, and I long stroked her. She had a round bubble bottom, gave good head, and satisfied me after she had gotten off of work around seven o'clock. After staying up talking to Tamera, whose nickname was 'Sunshine' the majority of her shift, I found out that she was a cool girl and a freak too. I'd have to keep in touch wit' her even when I got back home.

"Don't forget about me when you go back out of town, Sayveon," she said putting her uniform back on shortly after ten o'clock that morning.

"I ain't gonna do that, Li'l Mama," I promised.

She leaned over the bed where I was laying and gave me a kiss on the lips. "Be good and have a safe trip."

"I'll hit you up when I get back."

"Alright. I'll be expecting that call."

"Don't get in no trouble wit' your job. You sure you straight wit' that?"

"I told you, I'm good, baby. That's my homegirl downstairs at the desk that took over the new shift. She's not going to tell nobody. We're close friends, so I'm not worried."

"That's what's up."

She walked out and closed the door behind her. I prob'ly wouldn't be able to count how many other playas stepped through the hotel that she and her girl had fucked, but I wouldn't judge her. I had banged it, and there were no strings attached. She was just another one that I had hit, but I would try to stay in contact because I liked her company, and she gave good head. After a full conversation, I had her in there freakin' me down. I couldn't help it. The way I talked to a bitch could convince her to go to hell and sell snow-cones. The technique I used to mack and break a hoe was cold as ice.

I got up and showered before calling my cousins to see if they were ready to dip out and head back home. The partying was over, and now it was time to handle what needed to be handled. I was more than ready to murk a mothafucka and retaliate on er'body that I had an issue wit'. It would be a killing spree that 'The Sipp' had never seen before.

Three Hours Later

Sparkle

Mama V had called me about an hour earlier telling me that she was out of town visiting her niece who had just had a babygirl. She was on her way back and wanted me to go over to her place and check things out. I called Sayveon and asked him if he would go over there with me just to make sure that everything was good. We arrived about the same time and both got out.

"So, she just said that he ain't answering the phone?" Sayveon asked. He looked me up and down. I knew he couldn't resist glueing his eyes to my thick hips and plump li'l cute tits no matter how he tried to play hard.

"Yes," I answered back, checking him out. He was almost irresistible standing there fully clad in his thugged out gear lookin' like a trap star. I moved all of my horny thoughts to the back of my mind and tried to concentrate on the reason that we were there.

Sayveon and I walked up to the door. He knocked and knocked on the door, but there was no answer. We stood there waiting to see if Mr. Travis would eventually come and open up for us. Then, I heard moaning and groaning. I sucked my teeth because I figured that while Mama V was gone, he had brought some ratchet in their house.

"You know what? I don't have time for this shit right here. He ain't answering because he's in there messing around on her, and this right here ain't even cool," I said, firing off.

The next thing that we heard was something fall to the floor. I put my head up to the window trying to listen and see what the hell was going on up in there.

"If he is in there wit' a broad, that's on him. I ain't trying to get in their shit. I'ma stand here for a few more minutes then I'm bouncing," Sayveon said.

"He better not have another woman in there because she said she was on her way here."

We both turned around when we heard someone coming up. It was Mama V driving up in her car. She hopped out quickly and ran up to us nervously putting her key in the keyhole to get inside. "Thank you both for coming. I've been calling him all day, and I can't understand why he won't return my calls."

What I saw when she opened the door was enough to make my stomach flip over and over again. I could hardly stand there from the disgusting sight of it all. WTF!

Just Horrible

Sparkle

Mama V yelled out a loud, whooping cry. Mr. Travis was laid sprawled on the floor, severely disabled and disfigured. There was about a two-inch hole in the heel of his swollen right foot. He had no nose, only a red, raw, exposed septum, surrounded by a narrow opening. His right eye was lying right beside him and a large dark spot sat where his eyeball should have been. The skin on his face drooped from having so many broken bones in it. On his right hand, his index, middle and ring fingers were stumps but the left hand was even worse. He had a funny looking hunk of flesh for a thumb, and the only other finger left was the pinky finger. Bloodstains covered the beige colored rug and Mr. Travis' body.

"Honey, can you hear me?" Mama V asked him.

He didn't respond. He just laid there. Mama V dropped to her knees crying and hollering out in sorrow.

"Call for help," I told Sayveon as I walked out of there. I couldn't stand to look at him like that any longer. He had been slaughtered and treated like he wasn't human.

A young black neighbor next door came out of her place. "Is everything alright?" she asked me. Apparently, she had heard the screams and cries of Mama V.

"Have you seen anything strange going on around here or anyone comin' out of here?" I asked her hoping I could get some answers.

"Well, I left earlier, and when I got back, I was coming up the sidewalk and saw a black man in a hoodie with two dogs that looked like American Bulldogs. One was black and the other was brown and the guy came out of there. I had never seen him before, but I thought maybe it was the couple's son or relative."

"Was he driving or walking?"

"He drove a white pick-up truck. I'm not sure what kind. I didn't pay him much attention."

"Okay, are you willing to tell what you saw?"

"Sure. Why what happened in there?" Her whole facial expression changed to a worried one.

"Mr. Travis is down on the floor, and from the looks of it, he might not make it. Whoever came in here earlier today had those dogs to tear him up."

"Is it that bad?"

"Hell, yeah."

When Mama V came out, she was still in tears and barely able to catch her breath. "Why would someone do this to him? We don't bother anyone," she said between sobs.

The neighbor looked at me with sadness. "I'm going in, and if you need me, knock."

"Okay."

This was a hard one to figure out because the house was still in order and nothing had been stolen or disshuffled. Whoever caught him wanted him dead, and it seemed to be some kind of revenge. I couldn't think of a single person that he could have had a problem with except for Pops. But, Pops was in the hospital recovering from his surgery. The last I had heard, he was struggling to recover. It was a mystery that I couldn't solve, but at least a witness came forward.

After Getting It On

Stephanie

I stared into the eyes of Tank who rubbed my hair gently and held me in his arms. The sex was all that I thought it would have been. The dick had me dumb because he knew how to please a woman. I loved that about him and liked how he put it down in the bedroom.

"I need to go and hit these streets, gotta grind, baby," Tank said.

"Don't get hurt out there doing nothing," I told him out of concern.

"I'm good. I ain't new to this shit."

We got up, showered, and put our clothes back on. He grabbed me from the back and hugged me tightly. He kissed me on the back of the neck and made a smile creep across my face. I was so into him, and each time that we met up, I found myself falling more and more for him.

"Before you leave, I got you somethin' special." He walked over to the closet, opened it, and pulled out an extra large burgundy leather Michael Kors handbag and gave it to me. "This is just a li'l gift that I picked up for you the other day."

My mouth dropped. I was totally surprised. "You kno' how to put a smile on my face. Thank you baby for thinking of me." I gave him a kiss on the lips, but that wasn't enough for him. He opened his mouth and slid his tongue in mine, and we had a passionate kiss.

"Call me later on."

"I will. I'm planning to go and check on my auntie while I'm down here and see how she's making it."

"Let me kno' how she's doing."

"Will do."

Tank followed me to the car and watched me get in and slide behind the wheel. He then got in his ride and we drove off in opposite directions. My entire ride was filled with thoughts of Tank and how much I had begun to like him. It seemed as though I was finally getting my life back and had found someone special who would treat me right.

Hell Of A Day

Stephanie

Aunt Ruby had been moved to a regular room and out of the Intensive Care Unit. Boy was I happy and excited to see her conscious and in her right state of mind. She still wasn't all the way well, but at least things were lookin' better for her.

I stood over her. "Hey, there. How are you feelin' today?"

She slowly smiled and whispered, "I'm doin' pretty good. My life was spared, and I'm blessed to be in the land of the living."

"I kno' that's right."

"How's Sparkle and the baby doing?"

"Everyone is fine. We're worried about you gettin' well so that you'll be able to come home."

"I'm tryin'."

I leaned over and hugged her gently. "I love you, Auntie Ruby."

"I love you, too."

Not having her around made me realize how important it was to live everyday like it was my last. Her drowsy lookin' eyes and weak voice were signs of her struggle to make it through what had been thrown at her. She was the type of woman who wouldn't give up easily, and I admired her for that. I stroked my fingers through her silky hair and took a deep breath. I could breathe with ease knowing that she would be okay.

As I gazed down into her pretty dark brown eyes, I felt the need to tell her what was placed on my heart to say.

"Auntie, thank you for believing in me and never turning your back. You inspire and motivate me to do better. I've been through a lot, but that doesn't mean that I'm goin' to give up. Heroin ruined my life and took away time from my boys that I can never get back. I stole from my mother and did some stuff in the streets that I'm too shame to even repeat."

"It's okay, and you'll be just fine." She cleared her throat and coughed a few times. "You don't have to explain a thing to me, Chile. I'm not here to judge you."

"I kno'. But, I want to tell you this while we're both still living. I may not get this opportunity again. I don't want to pass it up."

"Go ahead, baby. I'm listening," she said in a low tone.

"You've taught me how to stay strong and not go back to my old ways. I took advantage of my mother while she was living and kicked her to the backside. I borrowed money from her and didn't give it back. Mama loved me regardless of what I did and never clowned me and called me out of my name. I felt small when people in the streets would call me a junkie and smackhead. While in rehab, I wanted to kill myself a few times because I didn't want to go through the withdrawals of being without it. I have enough willpower to go on and remain strong now. I want to tell you thanks. Thanks for being the mother that I no longer have, and thanks for being understanding. Most people wouldn't have ever talked to me because of my past."

I held back the tears and gave her a warm smile. She reached for my hand and placed it over her heart. "You'll always have a special place right here, li'l girl."

Our conversation was rudely interrupted when one of the old Evan sisters from Aunt Ruby's church marched right in. The oldest one of the women, Rose spoke, "God is good."

"Hello, how are you?" I asked although I was annoyed that she busted in like that.

"I'm blessed by the best."

"Good."

I kissed Aunt Ruby on the side of her face and told her, "I'm gonna go on to the house and let you talk to your company. Tell one of the nurses to call the house phone if you need anything. I'm gonna be there for a li'l while. It's a long story, but we'll talk about all of that when you get back."

"Stay as long as you need to. You're always welcomed there," she spoke softly. I went on and let her and her church member visit with one another.

Seeing her alert had made my day. I wouldn't know what to do if something happened to her.

***

I attempted to start the car but the old bucket wouldn't even crank. I tried a second time and still, no luck. Dammit! I slid over and got out and slammed the door behind me. I was sooo pissed off. I went back to the hospital room.

"Auntie, your car won't start. It may need a battery."

"It may be time for a new one," she let me know.

"I'll take you home," Rose offered.

"I'd appreciate it if you would."

"I have some battery cables at the house," Aunt Ruby said.

"Alright. When Sparkle comes home, I'll get her to bring me back down here and get your car. I'll get a new battery put in," I told her in order to ease her mind and not have her worrying over that.

"Well, Ruby I'll come back on another day and see you, but you may be going home soon. You look like you're doing a whole lot better. I'll keep you in my prayers, and the church has you on the prayer list," Rose said.

"Tell everybody that I said I hope to be back there as soon as possible," Aunt Ruby replied.

I was riding with Rose lost in my own thoughts as she zoomed her red Lincoln MKZ down the street. The sound of police sirens pulled me out of my thoughts and I looked around. The police car was right behind us. I glanced over, Rose was going 65 miles per hour, and the speed limit was only 45. This was beginning to be one of the worst days of my life. Why was she driving that fast anyway at her age?

"Oh, sweet Jesus! There is a police behind me, so I guess I better pull over," she said and pulled the car over to the right side of the highway.

A handsome young black cop stepped up to the vehicle. "Ma'am, you were going over the speed limit. I'm gonna need your driver's license and insurance."

"I'm sorry officer, but it got taken away from me two years ago for drunk driving."

My eyes grew bigger than a volleyball. I could hardly believe what had come out of her mouth.

The cop's entire demeanor changed, and he looked away like he didn't quite know what to say and then looked right back at her. "Well, let me see your registration for your car," he stated.

"I stole this car from my friend, choked him, and tossed him in the damn trunk." This lady was plain ole' nuts. I always got tied up in strange bullshit like this. I thought she was supposed to be a Christian!

He spoke into the walkie-talkie attached to his shirt. "I am going to need some help out here off of the Nissan Parkway. In need of some backup."

"Why do you need to call somebody for me, I'm an old senior?" Rose had jacked up my day with her crazed butt. I actually sat in the car with a straight lunatic. This lady was cray cray!

"I need for both of you to step out of the car and put your hands on the hood for me," he ordered furiously.

We both got out and put our hands on the front of the car and waited for back up to arrive. Five minutes later, half of the squad showed up. My heart thumped at a fast speed from nervousness, frustration, and lots of anger. I could possibly be charged because I was riding wit' the fool, and I didn't even kno' what the hell was goin' on.

The first cop who pulled us over in the beginning stepped over to another one and told him exactly what Rose had said to him. The deputy walked over to Rose and said, "I need to see your license and registration, Ma'am."

"If you hand me my purse off the front seat, I'll get it for you, and the paper that you need is in the glove compartment."

The deputy grabbed all of the stuff from the ride and brought it back over to her. "Get your license out for me."

She dug in the purse and pulled it right out. They then ran the license plate number and made sure that everything was legit. The deputy popped the trunk and flinched. I knew we both were going to jail. My whole world stopped.

"There's nothing back here and everything came back clean," the deputy said.

Rose cocked her finger at the cop that started the commotion. "That liar. I bet he lied and told you that I was speeding too, huh?"

"Ignoring what she had said, the deputy told her that she could go and to be careful."

She went through all of that in order to dodge a damn speeding ticket. It was funny. At first, she had me damn near 'bout to piss on myself.

When she dropped me off, I thanked her for the ride even though it still had me somewhat shaken up. "You're welcome, girlie." She laughed. "I had them going didn't I?"

"Yes, you did." As I was about to go in the house, I heard several shots that sounded like a shotgun.

The old lady let her window down. "Don't let that scare you. That's Ontavious down there hunting."

"Oh. Okay." I went inside mumbling to myself , "What a ride home." She needed to go and apply for an S.S.I. check for that stunt she pulled earlier. I'm sure she'd qualify for a crazy check, but she did get out of paying that speeding ticket. I giggled to myself thinking about what she had done. I was glad I made it home and didn't find myself in a cell. Guess she played a good joke on me along with the po-pos.

Gotta Hold On

Sayveon

The man who I considered my father the majority of my life had been wheeled out on a stretcher and covered wit' a sheet. I didn't want to feel any pain because we weren't close, and it wasn't always good between us. I did though. Finding out that he wasn't who I thought he was, was somewhat of a surprise. It damaged me a li'l to kno' that I wasn't the genetic offspring of William Travis. The person officially recognized as my dad.

I sat in my whip in front of Mama's crib. I was zoned out remembering how thangs weren't always bad between Dad and me. I could recall being a li'l dude 'bout nine or ten and us spending time outside playing basketball on the court he made for me. He taught me how to dribble the ball and play the sport that I grew to love and would still play off and on when I found the time to. He attended my middle and high school graduation and went to work every day to provide for his family and help out wit' the bills. Mama and him both worked hard and then retired after so many years. Yet in still, I never felt a connection wit' him and felt that he never showed me much love. I always felt that there was a distance between us.

He never told me that he was proud of me, and sometimes he acted like I wasn't his. I now know why. I wasn't. He knew that I wasn't his son, and he never had kids of his own. When I got older and got hard headed, I left the house. I got out on my own and started hustling. I was out there, doin' my thang. He didn't agree wit' it, so we eventually stopped speaking altogether.

I wished thangs could have been different between us, but they weren't. I looked up and wondered whose car was sitting right in front of mine wit' a Georgia license plate. The only person I knew who lived there and would come and visit every blue moon was Uncle Theon. Wit' a lot on my conscious, I made my way into the crib where the cuzzo's were huddled up in the front area conversing back and forth.

Uncle Theon stood up and spoke. "Hey, nephew."

"Long time since I've seen you," I said to him.

"Well, I wish it was under better conditions. My daughter got killed, and her mother wants to go ahead and have a funeral service for her tomorrow with family and friends and then bury her," he let out in a saddened way. He dropped his head down and let out a deep breath. "I'd appreciate it if all of you all would come. Menace 'nem say they will stay an extra day or two so that they can attend. Will you be able to make it?"

"You kno' I got you fam. I'm sorry to hear 'bout this. If y'all need anything, be sho' to let me kno', and I'll help out wit' whatever it is."

Menace, Viscious, and Bone agreed wit' what I had said and told him that they were there for him too.

He was my mother and their mother's baby brother who we rarely saw. He left and moved to Georgia when I was about two years old. I knew that he had a daughter who lived in Jackson, but I had never met her before. I don't think she even talked to him much. Her mother married another dude, and the girl kind of went her own way and didn't contact Uncle Theon much.

"Mama, I need to holla at you," I told her and stepped into her bedroom.

She came strutting in. "What is it?"

"You may want to sit down for this one."

With a look of confusion, she took a seat on the bed and anxiously looked at me, ready for me to let her kno' what the deal was. "I'm listening."

"Today, Daddy got murked. Somebody ran up on him wit' dogs. The dogs tore him to pieces. I mean, his face was destroyed. I don't kno' who is behind it, but the po-po 'pose to be investigating and looking for fingerprints," I revealed sympathetically.

She was dazed and staring at me wit'out blinking. "My chest is feeling tight." Mama placed her hand on the upper part of her body and gasped for breath.

I lifted her up to the top of the bed. "Lay right here and rest. I made sure the pillows were properly prompted under her head, went to the kitchen, and got her a glass of ice water. I could hear loud screams and sobs comin' from her. I knew that she mourned the loss of the man she had been wit' for years and years. Even though the divorce papers had been signed and turned back in to the attorney, it hadn't been finalized. That meant one thang, she would have to plan the funeral of the dude who left her to be wit' another woman.

Uncle Theon ran in where I was. "Sis just told me that William was killed, damn."

"Yeah, I wanted to tell her in private and make sho' she would be a'ight."

"I understand. I don't kno' what's goin' on. Death is knockin' down doors 'round here. You kno', my daughter's death was a shock to me, and I still can't believe it. We weren't very close, but I wish I would have had a better relationship with her."

I nodded. "You gotta be strong and deal wit' what's goin' on now. You can't change the past, Unc." I flipped subjects. "What happened to her, anyway?"

"Sudden accident. I can't talk about it without shedding a tear." His eyes watered up, and he walked away and went outside.

I took the glass of water to Mama, lifted her head, and helped her drink. She had gotten weak and her hands were shakin'. "Lay back down. I'll come back and check on you."

Menace stepped in. "Er' thang good, Cuz?" he wanted to know. To keep Mama calm, I moved in the hallway and told him what all had happened. He felt some kind of way about it all too because he visited and called him Uncle William.

I went to my room and peeped in on Janay and Layla. They were sound asleep. Seeing my girl's faces was the highlight of my day. I never wanted nothin' to ever happen to either one of 'em. I needed to be 'round to protect 'em, but the way shit was poppin' off, I wondered if I'd be the next one to fall. Shit was fucked up, and it would only get worse before it got any better.

Shocked And Distressed

Sparkle

Stephanie told me that Aunt Ruby was in a regular room and feeling better. I stopped by to see her but only stayed a short while because I was so shaken up from what I had seen earlier. All I could picture in my head was Mr. Travis laying there on that floor, lifeless. Bloodstains filled the carpet. I don't think a person could have died in a more horrifying and gruesome way. I didn't ever expect to walk in on that. I had never seen anything like it.

My hand still quivered each time the image of him came into my head. I couldn't even enjoy my visit with Aunt Ruby because I was too antsy and uneasy. At least I did get some good news that day though. She would eventually make a full recovery and be able to come back home. When I got to the country I didn't see Aunt Ruby's car where it usually sat and figured that Stephanie must have been gone somewhere else after she visited her earlier that day. I tried to get out, but I was too weak and my body wouldn't move. I was completely drained.

"What's taking you so long to get out?" Stephanie peeped her head out of the door and asked.

"Come here."

She came on out and gave me the weirdest look. "Girl, you look like hell. What's wrong with you?"

I had cried so long and hard before I made it that I prob'ly did look like shit. "I've been to hell and back.

Mr. Travis was killed. Me, Sayveon, and Mama V walked in and found him dead. Mama V asked me to go over and check on him because he was not answering her calls. I called Sayveon to come meet me because I didn't feel comfortable going by myself. When we got there, I knocked and banged on the door but he didn't answer. At one point I heard moans coming from the inside, so I thought he was in there with another woman. Sayveon said he was going to knock one more time and then leave because he didn't want to be involved if Mr. Travis was in there with another woman. Before we could leave, Mama V pulled up, and we went in. Soon as we walked in, there he was, laying on the floor in a pool of blood." I sighed and finished telling her all about it.

I grabbed my cell and browsed through it until I found the pictures I had taken of Mr. Travis and then handed the phone to Stephanie. "Oh, shit!" she cried out. I sneaked and took it while nobody was watching. The picture showed Mr. Travis on his back in a pool of blood. His hands were taped in front of him. Part of his face had been torn apart, and it was sunken in. He also had a bloody lip with puncture and bite marks on his temple and the top of his head. A big hunk of his ear, part of his nose, a few fingers, and an eye were missing. There were also punctures from where the beasts sunk their teeth into his arms.

Stephanie immediately tossed the phone back to me and began breathing hard. She stared down at the ground for a while before helping me into the house. All I wanted to do was lay down and sleep for the remainder of the day. I didn't have any sleep medication, but I had a package of Benadryl on my nightstand. I normally take them every now and then for my allergies. Since they make me sleepy, I only took one and closed my eyes.

Stephanie peeped in to check on me. "Do you need anything?" she asked.

"No. I'm alright."

I felt depressed and wanted to isolate myself from everyone, and I was sure that Mama V had to be feeling the same way. When I got better, I'd have to try to meet up with her. I knew she needed some consoling.

While murder is always horrific, this was one of the few cases that was more blood-curling than others. I wouldn't have wished what happened to Mr. Travis on my worst enemy.

Clearing My Head

Sayveon

My uncle, cousins, and I drank beer and talked in the den while Mama rested in her room. We went back and forth trading stories about our younger days.

"I've had more women than I can count," Uncle Theon bragged as he cocked his leg up on the arm of the sofa. "Y'all young boys can't tell me shit about pulling a broad. I used to have more women than I did money." He laughed, and we chuckled too. We all let him have his moment. I didn't interrupt him even though I figured he was lying on his dick. I knew how niggas lied, so it didn't bother me none.

"Uncle Theon, 'bout how many could you knock down in the same day? I can beat down at least three and still go strong when I get to my main ole' lady," Bone boasted. He took a sip from the can, laughing his ass off. I didn't pay him no mind either. I knew Bone could tell more lies than the devil himself.

I had Layla on my lap holding her, and Janay watched cartoons in another room. My baby leaned over toward the beer. She was whining, wanting to taste some. "Nope, you can't have none of this," I objected and passed her her bottle from the table in front of me. Still, I had my ear tuned in to the conversation.

"Man, I could sleep with 'bout three women at the most and still have a rock hard one," Unc said. He hopped up from his seat and stood up straight. "My dick would still be standing up as straight as I am now."

I was sitting there listening to them talk shit when I realized that I needed to check the mail at my crib. I interrupted, "I'ma go and check my mail back at my place. I'll be back in a li'l while."

"Go ahead. We'll be right here waiting for you when you get back," Unc said.

I took the girls to my Mama and assured her that I'd be right back. I needed to get some fresh air and relieve a li'l stress by bustin' a few blocks. On the ride there, I wondered to myself who had gone up in there and killed Daddy. I wondered if maybe Mama V had it all set up, but, she wouldn't have had a reason to pull no shit like that. I also doubted if Pops was behind it because he was too sick to be plotting and having anybody killed. I didn't have a clue who did it. I wished that I had been dreaming, but it was reality. Shit had been gettin' real lately.

Last Words To Me

Sayveon

When I got to the house, I pulled in the driveway and got out to get the mail. I got back in my car and sorted through it all. Most of it was bills, and I had a couple of letters. I ran across a big brown envelope. The envelope was addressed to me and came from my dad. I wondered what could be inside since Do Not Fold was written on the front of it. I opened it and pulled out the paper inside. The letter read:

Be A Better Man Than Me

Son, I know that we've made a mends and are trying to work out our differences. This letter may seem mushy to you but hear me on out. Don't be like me and live life with little emotion and trying to be tough so others won't think that you're soft. You have a heart that's tender and giving. Tap into that power and show your loved ones that it's not all logic.

I've always tried to be a problem solver and searched for answers in reason. Now, I've learned that a simple hug can solve a lot of problems. Learn to use your heart and mind as one. What's really important is living your life to the fullest. Live one that is full of love because tomorrow isn't promised. Look at my life and how it's been filled with turmoil. I constantly searched for answers in all the wrong places. I want you to go in the right direction and take care of your two beautiful daughters. Steer them in the right direction too, and remember this- I'm here for you, I'm your friend, I'm your role model, and most important- I'm your dad.

Love Dad,

William

Behind the letter was a picture of him and me when I was five years old. We both posed shirtless, holding out our muscles, smiling for the camera. I remember takin' it in the backyard and Mama snapping it. He had gotten it enlarged. On the back he signed it. *You'll always be my son!*

All kinds of emotions built up inside of me. It all seemed so unreal. I couldn't believe that he was gone. I was hurting inside but I knew I'd have to accept the death of my dad like a soldier.

Turmoil Might Be Over

Stephanie

After hearing Sparkle's phone ring non-stop for a few minutes, I went in there to check on her. She was so sleepy and drowsy that she opened her eyes, looked at me, and shut them right back. Her body was so sensitive to medication that even the lowest dosage of it would have her dazed out. I noticed her phone on the bed and picked it up just as it started to ring again.

The caller I.D. showed Sayveon's name and number on the screen so I answered, "Hey, Sayveon. This is Stephanie. What's up?"

"I kno' that Layla was supposed to stay until tomorrow, but we have had two deaths in the family. I was wondering if I could bring her down there."

"Well, Sparkle is sleeping right now. Hold on and let me ask her if it's okay."

"A'ight."

When I shook Sparkle, she barely opened her eyes. "Sayveon wants to know if he can bring the baby back today."

"That's fine," she slurred. "Leave me alone, heifer. I'm trying to sleep."

I put the phone back to my ear and gave him the address to put in his GPS to find us. "I'm on my way in a few minutes."

I told him ok and then hung up. I knew I would probably have to watch my niece until Sparkle came to her senses, so I went in the kitchen and made a pitcher of my favorite drink. After I poured me a glass of iced tea, I went in the living room to wait on Sayveon to drop Layla off.

A few hours had passed before I heard a car pull into the driveway. When I heard a car door slam, I got up and looked out of the window. Sayveon had Layla in his arms walking toward the house. I went out on the porch and greeted them. When Sayveon got close to me, I grabbed Layla and gave her a big hug. "Auntie missed you, li'l woman," I told her. She looked back at her daddy while sucking on her pink pacifier. Her curly jet-black hair had been neatly parted and put in li'l puffs. She looked so cute in her pink overalls with a white long sleeved shirt under it. On her feet she rocked some pink and white Bobs.

"You been doing a'ight?" he asked.

"I can't complain. Sparkle told me about your father. I want you to know that you have my condolences."

He dropped his head for a second. "It's a hard pill to swallow. Gotta keep on goin' though. Its gon' get better. He flipped topics, "I ain't never met y'all Auntie before or been way out here, but she has a nice place."

"She's recovering from a diabetic coma. Hopefully, she'll be coming home soon."

"Tell Sparkle to hit me up if she needs me." He kissed his daughter's cheek. "Love you my Li'l Momma."

The baby smiled at him and shyly placed her head on me. He was about to turn and go when a truck pulled into the yard. It was Ontavious, and I had a pretty good idea that all hell was about to break loose.

"You kno' them?" Sayveon asked, looking suspicious and raising a brow.

"That's our neighbor from down the road. I'll see you later." I tried to rush him off, but it seemed as though he already knew who he was by the frowns in his face.

"I kno' who that nigga is now."

Ontavious must have spotted Sayveon too because he backed out of the yard and left. Sayveon hopped in his vehicle, and I went in the house. I assumed that the confusion had died down between them and they both dropped it and went their separate ways. I was proud of Ontavious for being the better person in that situation. I didn't like the way either of them had treated Sparkle, but her child's father had done way more dirt than Ontavious. In the end, I had to trust her to be with whoever made her happy and try to mind my own business. She was smart enough to make up her mind without my help.

I played with the baby until she fell asleep in my arms. Being around her made me want a li'l girl. I laughed in my head at the thought of me having another baby, wishful thinking.

Long-Lost Cuzzo

Sayveon

The following Monday me and the fam met up wit' the cortege to pay our respects to Uncle Theon's daughter. We traveled from Kimberly's mother's house to New Hope Baptist church on Watkins Drive in Jackson. Hundreds of people gathered to pay their respects to the young woman who had lost her life. Kimberly's pink coffin, which had 'Angel' on the side, was carried in a horse-drawn carriage. Behind it, there was a car decorated wit' pink ribbons and flowers that spelled out, 'Daughter.'

When we got to the church, the pallbearers carried Kimberly's body in. After they opened the casket, we were given the opportunity to view her body. I figured out who Kimberly's mother was because she was the first person to go up and view the body. When she looked into the casket, she started crying and almost fainted. Next, I saw someone who I knew from the past go up and view the body. I wondered why she was even there. When I finally made it to the casket and looked down, I was shocked at what I saw. Her eyes were closed and she wore a pink dress. Her hair was in an updo wit' a bang. Her face had been covered wit' heavy make-up, and she appeared slightly swollen but it was clear who it was laying in that coffin. It was LaShune.

My feet couldn't move. I stood there for a minute. I rubbed my hand down the side of my face. The interior of the casket had an embroidered nameplate that read, Kimberly LaShune Montgomery. I put the pieces of the puzzle together and figured out why Nakia was the second person to view the body before taking a seat next to her mother. I realized that I had been standing there too long, so I shook my head and then went to sit wit' my fam. Shit was gettin' crazier by the day. Not only did I mistakenly fuck my own sister, I just realized that I had fucked my cousin as well. Ain't that some shit.

Out And About

Sparkle

Getting Mama V out for the day was a hard thing to do. She eventually agreed, and we met up at the Food Court of Northpark Mall and ate Chick-fil-A. She dressed neat as usual, but I could tell from her make-upless face, bags underneath her red eyes, and constant yawning that she hadn't been to sleep. She was depressed, and it showed.

I bit down on the chicken sandwich and then chewed a few fries. "How you been holdin' up?" I asked her.

"Not well. I miss him so much. It's been really hard. I haven't slept since it happened. I still can't understand why someone would have done him that way."

"Me either. Maybe the police will be able to find out what went on. Do you think Pops might have been involved?" I knew that I prob'ly shouldn't have asked that question, but I did.

"I'm unsure if he had any involvement. I haven't spoken to him since the night he ruined my party."

"Maybe someone will be caught in due time."

Mama V sipped soda from a straw before eating a waffle fry dipped in ketchup. "I don't have an appetite."

"Don't try to force yourself to eat then. It's okay."

She rubbed her tiresome eyes. "I'm worried about what's going to happen with the funeral. His wife is still legally over the planning of it. I mean, she signed the papers. Everything was turned in, but nothing has been finalized."

"Try not to worry over that because it's something that you have no control over. It'll all work itself out."

"I'm sure she hates me though. Yet, she had a son by my husband, and she acts like she is the only one who is supposed to be upset." Her face had started to turn red, and her hand trembled.

I reached over and patted her on the arm. "It's going to be fine. Let it go. You loved him, and he loved you. Think about the days that you were blessed to be able to share with him. Let all of that other nonsense go."

"Put yourself in my shoes, Sparkle. If it were you, you'd be troubled too. It's hard not to be. I was finally blessed with a man who cared about me. William and I vacationed and spent time together. He listened to me and understood the person that I am. We felt so right. We both dreamed of spending our lives together and growing old side-by-side. All of that has been taken away from me." She held her head down and took a deep breath.

I knew that she was saddened and exhausted at the same time. "Let's go," I said. I didn't even finish what I was eating. I just tossed it in the garbage.

We decided to do some shopping and ended up in Dillard's Department Store. Mama V was all smiles. I knew she loved to shop until she was about to drop. She tried on several different outfits until she found a few that fit her just right. One dress that she put on had a tie up-bow in the back. "Sparkle," she called out.

"Uh-huh," I answered.

"I need you to come and tie this up for me, please."

As soon as I stepped in to help her, her cell went off. She put up one finger, telling me to give her a moment to answer it. She began talking, and from her frowns and sighs, I knew it had to be from someone that she didn't want to hear from. I sat on the small bench in the dressing room and waited for her to finish her conversation. I ain't gonna lie. I was earhustlin' and being straight nosey. I recognized the voice on the other end of the phone, and I could clearly hear what was being said.

"Veronica, I'm going home today. I'm feeling a lot better, but I'm missing you baby," Pops confessed.

"Al, right now I'm going through a lot, and I don't want to discuss this with you."

"I heard all about your little boyfriend getting killed. Maybe it wasn't meant for you two to get married after all."

"How did you hear about that?" She held a puzzled look.

"Word travels, darling."

"I don't wish to rekindle anything with you, Al. For years I tried, and now I've given up."

"I'll get you back. Even if I die trying."

Mama V hung up and said, "I don't know what's getting into Al."

"What do you mean?"

"He's beginning to act like he's losing the little bit of mind that he had." She checked herself out in the mirror and flipped topics. "I love this. Tie it up for me please so that I can see what it really looks like."

While I was putting a bow in the strings, I couldn't help but wonder if Pops had Mr. Travis knocked off. I was beginning to think so. I would never speak on it again because some things are better left alone. I wasn't trying to get myself put in the midst of it by telling the authorities. I lived by the 'no snitching' code of the streets. My lips were sealed.

Saying The Final Goodbye

Sayveon

At the graveyard the family was seated right in front of the body, waiting to say their last farewells to LaShune and watch her go down into the dirt.

The preacher looked at the casket. "We therefore commit Kimberly LaShune Montgomery's body back to the ground; earth to earth, ashes to ashes, dust to dust; in the sure and certain hope of the Resurrection to eternal life."

Two black city cemetery employees then lowered her into the grave. As she was goin' down, the lowering device broke. The casket slid at an angle into the grave. It hit the side of the vault, and came to rest in the grave at an angle. The impact of it hittin' the side of the vault made the lid disconnect and exposed LaShune's body.

One of the workers appeared visibly shaken and said, "Oh my God! Hold on! We're sorry about this. We will fix the problem."

"I know good and damn well that you better. You two bastards gonna have the biggest lawsuit that you've ever seen before when I'm done with you!" LaShune's mother yelled while crying hysterically. She hopped up and attempted to go and confront the worker, but the funeral home director stopped her.

When the two tried to lift the box from the grave, the bottom separated from the sides causing the body to slide out the casket and into the bottom of the grave. The two workers took off, fleeing on foot. The family screamed after the men, but they kept running. Nakia had to be stopped by a few family members from trying to dive down in the ground with her sister.

"LaShune!" she shouted.

Four men from the crowd volunteered to help. They lifted LaShune by her legs and arms and placed her body on the ground. Family members took Nakia and her mother away. The funeral home assured them that the situation would be handled properly.

Mama held on to Uncle Theon, and we all walked off. All I wanted to do was get the hell away from there, go back to Mama's, and chill. Even in her death, LaShune still raised hell from the grave.

Time With My 'Boo'

Stephanie

Tank came and picked me up from Aunt Ruby's. I planned to spend a few nights at his house. It would be my first time ever going to his crib. I was happy because it meant that we were making progress. For him to invite me over meant that he trusted me and wanted our relationship to move further along.

"You want to stop and get a bite to eat?" he asked on the way there.

"No. I'm good for right now."

He reached over, held my hand up to his mouth, and gently kissed it. I blushed, hard.

It took about forty-five minutes to an hour for us to arrive at his spot. He lived on East Hill in Jackson, which was in an upscale community. Damn, it was beautiful from the outside! I got anxious wondering what the inside looked like. When he parked, I grabbed my overnight bag off the backseat and hopped out.

"Come on so I can give you a tour, baby," Tank said.

The inside of Tank's home was designed with high ceilings and gorgeous wood floors throughout. The rooms were also very large. After the tour of the inside, he led me outside where there were two covered porches. A granite pool was on one side, and a spa was on the other.

"This is so nice," I complimented.

Tank held me close and kissed me on the lips. "If you hang on in here wit' me, we can share this shit together. You only gotta show me that you're loyal and trustworthy. And, you can't bail out on me when times get hard. You gotta be down for the bad and the good."

"I can do that."

He led me to the master room and showed me four huge walk-in closets. "There is more than enough space to hold all of your gear and mine," he said. Then he showed me his bathroom. "I recently had the bathroom remodeled," he explained. It had been updated into a stunning modern design. It looked like a place to loosen up a tired mind and body after a long stressful day. It was a nice area to be isolated and relaxed in. I pictured myself being immersed in the bathtub, taking a bubble bath. It looked to be relaxation at its best. It had a spa-like ambience, and I loved it. I thought to myself, I can get used to this lavish lifestyle.

"I need to show you what our next move will be," Tank said with a huge smile.

He led me to the kitchen where he opened a drawer, pulled out a pamphlet, and passed it to me. "What is this?"

"Read it, girl."

It was travel guide information about Jamaica with pictures of the beautiful island in the Caribbean. I always wanted to visit the birthplace of the legendary reggae singer Bob Marley.

"I have always wanted to go there," I said.

"I need to kno' how you'd feel 'bout goin' wit' me before I ask my travel agent to go ahead and make arrangements."

I almost died right then and there. "I would love to baby."

I wrapped my arms around his neck and gave him the biggest bear hug that I could give. I felt so special. No man had ever taken me somewhere like that before. I was caught up in the moment when I heard, "Y'all mothafuckas kno' what time it is!"

We both instantly turned around to see a man about 6'3 or 6'4 in a black ski mask. He had an A-K 47 pointed at us. "Show me where the money and the dope at," he ordered.

"I ain't got no dope in here if that's what you're lookin' for. But, you can get the racks that I got," Tank tried to reason.

"Take me to it," the husky voiced man instructed.

Tank led him into the master bedroom to a huge black safe in one of the closets. He put in a code and it opened. There had to be at least one hundred thousand dollars in it. I figured that there was more somewhere else. From the way he lived that had to be only pocket change for him. No amount of money was worth our lives, so I was glad that he didn't put up a fight. He could get that cash back, but we couldn't get another life.

The stranger held up a black duffel bag. "Put all that goddamn money in it."

Tank did what he was told. I thought that would have satisfied the man and he would have left but it didn't. "You can have all of that, bruh. Gon' on and let me and my girl make it. I kno' this is part of the game and I ain't even mad," Tank said.

"Shut the fuck up, nigga!" His anger showed from the loudness of his voice. "Both of y'all drop down to yo' knees."

We got down. Having a gun pointed at me while I was powerless had me terrified as hell. I heard a loud bang and Tank fell flat on his face. Another round went off. I was shot in the back of my head, execution style. The bullet entered beneath my right ear and exited out of my throat. I fell forward, face first. I didn't feel myself hit the ground. Retrospectively, I was in shock.

I heard the front door shut, hard. When I saw blood on the white carpet, I panicked. A burning pain shot through my neck. Then I was wet, cold, and getting colder quickly. I became desperate for help and began gargling on my own blood. I began to lose consciousness and suddenly everything went dark.

Missing In Action

Sparkle

I hadn't seen, heard, or spoken to Stephanie since she got in the car with her new boyfriend. I was becoming worried. Besides, I didn't know Tank like that. He seemed like a cool dude, but people could be so deceiving that I didn't trust anybody. I had called Stephanie about six times that morning. My gut feeling told me that something was wrong.

I got Layla dressed and drove to the police station. I went inside and explained to the officer sitting at the front desk that my sister hadn't returned any of my phones calls. I wanted to file a missing persons report on her. The officer at the desk called another officer to come talk to me. After telling the officer my story he led me to his desk. When we got to his desk he sat down and told me to have a seat. He then gathered some paperwork together and began to ask for information about Stephanie.

"I am going to need a full description of your sister with a recent photograph. One from the waist up would be the best," he said. He acted so nonchalant that I was getting a li'l frustrated.

I gave him every detail that I could think of. He asked, "Does she have any tattoos?"

"No."

"What was she wearing yesterday?"

"A black leather jacket, long sleeved white shirt, black skinny leg jeans, and black shoes."

"Any birthmarks?"

"On her back she has a small heart. That's her birthmark."

"Who was she last seen with?" he asked, slowly looking up at me.

"This guy named Tank. I'm sorry, but I don't know his real name. I only met him twice."

He didn't respond to what I said. He just kept writing. I found a picture on my phone of Stephanie that we took together a few days before. Looking at her made my stomach queasy. We were so happy on the picture; both of us were cheesing. I was proud of her because she overcame her addiction. I could tell that she wanted to do better and she had. My big sister had gone from a junkie to a normal person full of love and lots of energy. She could be a bit much at times but that was my blood. Wherever she was I hoped that she knew how much her li'l sister and niece loved her.

"Send that picture from your phone to my e-mail so that I can have it and upload it." He gave me the e-mail address, and I emailed the photo.

"Alright, I'm going to turn in this report. If you learn of any more information, I need you to call me. Hopefully, your sister will be found quickly and before any harm happens. If she turns up on her own, notify me so that we can call off the search. If we find her, we may not be able to disclose her whereabouts because she is an adult. The only thing that we'd be able to say is she is safe unless she gives out permission to tell you where she is."

"I understand."

He gave me his business card and I stood to leave.

"Have a good evening and try not to worry," he said as I walked away.

It would be hard not to worry or lose sleep over Stephanie. I knew that it was not a part of her character to stay gone like that and not answer her phone. The feeling that I had in the pit of my stomach didn't sit right with me. I knew that my sister was in some kind of danger or had been harmed. I had to get to the bottom of it with or without help from the police.

On My Gangsta Shit

Sayveon

It was a damp, chilly, and quiet night. Menace and I posted up behind the lame nigga's crib. As we were waiting, we smoked on that presidential shit, some kush. We passed the 'L' back and forth gettin' higher than any bird ever flew.

About ten or fifteen minutes had gone by before we spotted headlights comin' up. We both reached for our heaters and took our positions. The dude turned the engine off and got out. We could hear him whistling a tune. I peeped from beside the corner of the house and then bomb rushed him to the ground.

"Ole punk ass nigga. You thought you couldn't be touched, but I got yo' bitch ass," I said to him.

I hopped up from the cold ground and aimed the heat at this head. "Please, don't do this," Ontavious begged wit' his hands up in the air. He laid on the ground huffin' and puffin'.

"Turn over, mothafucka," were my words to him.

He rolled over, and I let off two rounds in his ass. I had to get him back wit' that one. Shootin' or stabbin' a man in the ass took away some of his pride.

He grunted. "Argh. Come on, man. Let's let the animosity go."

"Nigga, I ain't lettin' what you did to me ride."

Before I could say another word, Menace let his tool bust off and blazed ole' boy's dome. His head dropped down to the cold ground and his movement completely stopped.

"Let's get the fuck away from here," Menace said.

We ran back to the old abandoned house up the road where I parked and jumped in. I cruised back to Jack-town knowin' that I had gotten sweet revenge.

***

Ginger was next on the hit list. I wouldn't stop until I put a bullet in her head. It seemed crazy that she had gotten her own crew and decided to take over the dope game. A dense blonde bimbo tryna call shots and push weight. Ha! I couldn't even picture it.

Our next stop was the apartment building where Ginger lived. The lot was full of cars and potential witnesses. I slowly crept by her place but her car wasn't there. No blinds were in the windows and it looked vacant. A Mexican man was next door to her smoking on a cig. I rolled the window down. "Amigo, is the white girl still living in that apartment next to you?"

To my surprise he spoke good English. "No, she moved out. I heard she bought a house somewhere."

I nodded. "Gracias." From being 'round Pops for so many years, I had picked up on the language. It was fucked up to kno' the bitch had moved. Now, I had to put out an APB on her and find out her whereabouts. She must've been doin' damn good to be able to move up in her own crib. She took what I had taught her and benefitted from it. Li'l did she kno', she was powerless in my eyes, and I planned to shut down her whole movement.

Troubles Are Doubled

Sparkle

The sound of my cell vibrating under my pillow interrupted my light sleep. I hadn't been able to fall into a deep one because I didn't know where Stephanie was. I would toss and turn all night until I drifted off.

"Hey," I said into the phone, knowing it was the Detectives number.

"This is Detective Bryan Gills."

"Yes. I know."

"Come on down to the station. I need to speak to you."

"I'm on my way."

I quickly changed Layla and got her dressed. I brushed my teeth and tossed on a pair of jeans and a hoodie. I hurried out of the door as fast as I could. On the way to the police station, I tried to think positive. I hoped that the detective had found Stephanie and she was safe. In my head, I pictured her sitting down waiting for me to come and take her home. Then, she'd have some type of silly story to tell me about some mess she had gotten herself trapped in. That was my big sister, always in the middle of some kind of foolishness. As long as she was safe, I would be fine.

When I got to the Police Department, I parked and quickly went inside. I stopped at the receptionist desk and said, "I need to speak to Detective Bryan Gills, please."

She picked up the phone and told him someone was there to see him. When he walked up he didn't greet me; he just motioned for me to follow him to his office. I had a feeling that the news wasn't good.

"Do you have a family member or friend who you may want to come down here with you?" he asked me.

"No. I only have an aunt but she's not in the best of health right now; she's in the hospital."

He rubbed his hand down his neatly trimmed sideburn. "We're investigating a double homicide. The body of your sister was found along with her boyfriend, 'Tank' whose real name is Deldrick Blackmon."

I gasped for air. "What happened to her?"

"She and the other victim were both shot in the heads. It was execution style. The bodies were found by the maid who went in to clean up this morning. I'm going to have to get as much information as I can from you. We want to solve these murders."

"I don't know much about him. I didn't even know what his real name was."

"Right now you'll have to go down to the morgue and identify the body."

I slowly got up, and he gave me the directions to the morgue. I walked away in denial. No, it ain't my sister. It has to be somebody else, I thought to myself.

The brick forensic morgue building looked scary and I kept saying to myelf that this was all a dream, that it couldn't be true. I called Ontavious three times and each time it went straight to his voicemail. I began to worry. This was very unusual. I needed him, and he was nowhere to be found.

I really didn't want to go in, but I knew I had to go. I got Layla from her car seat and walked into the building. I stopped at the front desk. The lady at the desk was reading a book and glanced up. "Hi, how can I help you?" she asked.

"I'm here to identify a body. I'm the sister of Stephanie Davis."

"Okay. It will be a few minutes. You can have a seat over there," she told me. I took a seat and tried calling Ontavious again. His phone still went straight to voicemail. A few minutes later, a short bald white man came out of a door at the end of the hall. "Hi. Are you a family member of Stephanie Davis?" he questioned.

"I'm her sister."

"Alright. Can I see your identification?"

I placed Layla in the empty chair beside me and got my license from the wallet inside of my purse. He examined it closely and then said, "Follow me."

He led me to the same door that he had come out of. He pressed the numbers on a key pad to enter his code to unlock the huge stainless steel door. The scent of antiseptic cleaning products made me almost vomit and the temperature was so cold that I shivered. I began to breathe shallowly. That made me even more sick and panicky. I wanted to hurry and get it over with so that my daughter and I wouldn't gag or worse, I would fall straight to the floor. I tried to relax and breathe normal. He guided me into a room. I looked at the body laying there on the gurney and nodded my head. It was indeed Stephanie. My head began to spin and the tears began to fall. I couldn't believe my big sister and best friend was gone. I felt as though I had died right along with her. I had to get out of there before I passed out.

I cried the whole way back home. I wanted to pretend that it was all a dream. I didn't know how I would break the news to Aunt Ruby. She was still in the hospital recovering from her own illness. I blamed Tank, and right then, I realized I hated him. Stephanie had no enemies. It had to be some bullshit he had going on that got her killed.

"I hate you!" I yelled out as if I was talking to Tank.

I had to pull over for a few minutes to get myself together. I used a few pieces of tissue to wipe my face. When I looked in the mirror, my blood red eyes overflowing with pain were looking back at me. My world suddenly felt different and unknown. It was now full of denial, anger, and depression. I didn't know how I was going to go on. How was I going to plan my sister's funeral and watch as she is lowered into the ground? I prayed for the Lord to give me strength so that I could be here for Layla and Aunt Ruby. In a sea of emotions, I put the car in drive, pulled out in the highway and headed home.

When I had gotten close to Aunt Ruby's, I spotted blue lights down the road. I was curious about what was going on, so I passed by her house and drove down the road. When I got closer, I pulled on the side of the road and parked because the street was blocked with police. Many neighbors stood on the side of the road talking and looking at the scene. My heart beat increased when I noticed that there was bright yellow plastic tape surrounding Ontavious' house. The words POLICE LINE DO NOT CROSS was written on the yellow tape. Men wearing black jackets with CID (Criminal Investigation Division) walked all around the premises and some wore gloves. Nervously, I grabbed Layla and got out of the car. I walked around searching for someone that I knew that I could ask what had gone on down there. I was frantic and felt like I would pass out with each step. First I had to deal with Aunt Ruby being sick in the hospital, then Stephanie being killed, and now this. I had a bad feeling that the police tape around Ontavious house was not good. I heard someone say, "Sparkle, come here, baby." I turned and looked in the direction of the voice. Rose, the oldest of the Evan sisters, was standing with the others, Retta and Rosalyn, and beckoning me to come join them.

I made my way over to them. "What happened? Why are so many police here? Where is Ontavious?" I had a lot of questions and needed answers fast.

They all looked at one another before Rose answered. "Ontavious has been killed. He didn't show up for work this morning, and his job called and reported it to the police."

It felt like I had been hit in the head with a brick. I couldn't take much more of the chaos that was starting to surround me. I screamed out and fell against the hood of Rose's car. One of them took Layla from my arms while I sobbed. I didn't look up to see which one. All of the sudden deaths were sucking the life out of me!

I'm Missing You

Sparkle

Mr. Travis, Ontavious, and Stephanie along with her boyfriend Tank all had been brutally murdered. All four of them had been buried in a week and a half. I still dealt with the grief of my sister long after the the funeral was over and the sympathy cards stopped coming. I grieved for her every day. The only thing that brought me comfort was knowing that she was with our parents. Dealing with her loss was hard for me, and I was glad that I had Aunt Ruby and Sayveon as a support system. When I needed encouragement and a listening ear Sayveon, had been there for me. He had been by my side since he found out about Stephanie's death. He even paid for her funeral.

Sayveon was there with me on the night of the Candlelight Memorial for Stephanie too. It was being held outside of Aunt Ruby's house. She was back at home and progressing from the diabetic coma. She helped me to plan the funeral and deal with all that was going on around me while trying to cope with all that had happened as well. I don't know what I would have done without Aunt Ruby and Sayveon.

In the middle of the yard, there were tons of stuffed animals, candles, and flowers. I was surprised at the number of people who showed. There had to be at least one hundred gatherers. Aunt Ruby's church had invited other churches to gather with us. I was so grateful that all of those people had come together to remember my sister.

With Sayveon beside me holding our daughter, I spoke holding a burning white candle. A picture of Stephanie smiling was centered to the right of me. I took a glimpse of it and quickly looked away to keep from breaking down.

"Thank you to everyone for being here and paying tribute to my sister. I know that many of you have had to travel a long distance in order to be here. It means so much to me and my family. Seeing so many loving people here is a reflection of how my sister's death has affected others. For those of you who don't know me, my name is Sparkle, and I'm Stephanie's younger and only sibling."

I was about to have a meltdown. I paused for a minute and Sayveon rubbed my shoulder. "Take your time, Sister," Aunt Ruby's preacher said.

After a few deep breaths, I continued. "Stephanie's outgoing personality made her a lovable person. She never met a stranger and could hold a conversation with anybody. She knocked down so many obstacles that stood in her way. She had become a great mother, sister, and friend. She taught me how to never give up. No matter what situation she had to cope with, she kept a positive attitude. I will miss her more than words can say. I'm glad that we got to spend so much time together and were so close. Her spirit will live on forever."

I cleared my throat. I hated to sing in front of people even though I knew I could blow. I did it for her. Brandy's lyrics of 'Missing You' rolled out of my mouth and sounded pure. "Though I'm missing you/I'll find a way to get through/Living without you/Cause you were my sister, my strength and my pride/ Only God may know why, still I will get by…"

As I sang, I noticed my nephews had arrived and were walking toward me. I reached out my arms while singing. They both walked right into my arms and stood with me. I know that their mother would have looked down at us and smiled. She would've been pleased.

Four Months After

Sparkle

Things had gotten a li'l better, but I still missed my sister. Not a day went by that I didn't think of her. I also thought about Ontavious and wondered why the two people who I truly loved had to die. The troubling thing to deal with was that they didn't just die; they were murdered. I couldn't think of one person that had a problem with Ontavious. The beef between him and Sayveon didn't go far; at least I didn't think it did. Plus, there was no way that Sayveon would have even known where Ontavious lived. I had a deep feeling that Stephanie's death was due to the shit that Tank had done in the streets. Hopefully, justice would be served.

It was now February 14th, and Sayveon offered to take me out to lunch. Aunt Ruby said that she would watch Layla, so I allowed him to come pick me up. He took me to LeFleur's Bluff State Park. When we got to the park, he called someone and from the tone of his voice, I assumed he was conducting business. I stared out lost in my own thoughts. I wasn't sure what was going on between us or what I wanted to happen. Sayveon hung up the phone, walked over to me, and put his arm around my waist. We held each other for a while taking in the scenery. A li'l while later, I heard sounds coming from behind me. When I turned around to see what it was I saw a catering service placing a red and white tablecloth on the table along with food. My heart melted, and I blushed. I thought that it was so sweet of him.

"I see you have a few tricks up your sleeves. I love it though," I said.

"Anything for you, baby."

We sat down at the table, which had been filled with different foods. There was fresh avocado dip and tortilla chips, deviled eggs, chicken macaroni salad, croissant club sandwiches, a large pitcher of fresh squeezed lemonade and green iced tea.

"I like this right here," I told him.

"Let's grub."

We began eating, but it didn't take long for me to get full off of all the good food. I wiped my mouth with a napkin and noticed Sayveon staring at me.

"What's the matter?" I asked.

"You're so damn beautiful, girl."

I waved him off. "Nigga, please. When you had all of this, you didn't even want it." I giggled behind my remark and drank from my cold glass of lemonade.

Sayveon grabbed my hand. "Let's put this food in the car and go for a walk on the trail."

When we were done putting the food up he locked the car, grabbed my hand, and we began to walk. I enjoyed the peaceful atmosphere. "I appreciate you being here for me. I kno' that our relationship was a rocky one. I put all of our differences aside, and I want to move forward and at least develop a good friendship with you," I said.

"Listen, baby." He stopped in his tracks and looked at me seriously. "I did some real fucked up shit in the past. Not having you and my baby girl made me realize how much I miss you. You were my other half and you cared 'bout me. Not because of my money or nothin' like that. You loved me even when I did some unforgivable shit. I ain't holdin' on to what we did to hurt each other. I want us to re-connect and make it work this time around."

"I think I would like that, but let's take it one day at a time. You'll have to show me that you've really changed," I said.

"I'll prove it to the world," Sayveon said as he stared into my eyes and rubbed my hand. There were several joggers out and a few people fishing in the huge body of water in front of us. I heard an airplane and looked toward the sky as it seemed rather low. I looked at Sayveon wondering if he had seen the plane as well. A young white lady walking stopped and gazed up in the air and said "OMG, look how sweet." When I looked at the sky again my heart began to do flip flops when I saw the words, SPARKLE, WILL YOU MARRY ME in the sky.

I was more than surprised. I didn't know how to even answer the question that he'd popped. Sayveon dropped down to one knee and held a beautiful diamond princess cut ring. It had to be at least four carats.

"Sparkle, I don't know where to even begin. I've tried so many ways to apologize that I'm runnin' out of options. You're the best that has ever happened to me. I want the world to kno' that I love you. I've made bad choices in my life that have affected us. I wanna change all of that. I didn't value your worth back then, but I gotta have you back because wit'out you I feel empty inside. You're my spine, and wit'out you, I'm paralyzed. I kno' I hurt you and words can't take that pain away… but maybe I can."

He held on to my hand and slid the ring on my ring finger. "I will never make stupid decisions again. My life is based on us. I've never felt this way 'bout nobody but you. I can't stand to see us just wither away. Let's water our love and watch it bloom again. Believe me when I tell you that I will never let anybody get in between us again. I wanna be dedicated to only you. I love every bit and ounce of you. Let me be your husband, and let's make it work. Will you be my wife?"

I had mixed feelings because Sayveon had proposed to me in the past. I rocked his ring but that didn't stop him from fuckin' around on me. For some reason, this time seemed different. "Yes, baby, I'll be Mrs. Travis," I said with excitement.

He hugged me tight, and I knew right then that all that we had gone through was to make him the man that I always believed he could be. It felt like it was all worth it. He had to lose me in order to appreciate me.

The Astonishing Paper

Sparkle

After Sayveon proposed, I felt like Queen Bee, like I was sitting on top of the world. Of course we were engaged before but he wasn't ready for marriage then, this time was different. Never had I dreamed that he would have made up his mind to change for the better. I also felt like the void that I felt had been filled a li'l. I knew it would take some time for it to completely fill because I had to go on without someone who meant a lot to me. My big sister wasn't there to enjoy this moment with me, and it hurt so much.

We walked back to the car, and Sayveon opened my door for me to get in. Once I got in, he walked around the car, got in, and pulled off. My leg began to itch, so I reached down to scratch it and noticed a piece of paper halfway under the seat. I picked it up to look at it and instantly felt lightheaded. It was LaShune's obituary. The words: THE HOMEGOING CELEBRATION OF MISS KIMBERLY LASHUNE MONTGOMERY was across the top of the paper with a photo of her smiling in the center.

I opened it up and read about her life. I closed it and put it back on the floor. "How did you know that she died?" I asked.

"Found out that she is my uncle's daughter. He came down for the funeral."

"Umph. So, is Nakia your sister too?"

"Nope."

"What happened to her?" I already knew the answer but still hoped to hear details.

"Heard that it was a car accident. A hit and run."

"Are they looking for the person that hit her?"

"I'on kno'." He shrugged his shoulders.

I didn't know how to respond after that. I felt horrible that me and Stephanie had acted up that night and were partially responsible for LaShune's death. I got scared and worried about what would happen to me if anyone found out the truth. I kept replaying in my mind all of the ways that I could have avoided that situation. I'd have to keep my head up, but it would be so hard for me to forgive myself.

Future Planning

Sayveon

"Where are we?" Sparkle wanted to kno' as we drove down through the country in a town called Raymond.

"We are heading to our new crib. I think it's best if we start over."

"Oh Lord, Sayveon, boy you are too much." She smiled from ear to ear. When we pulled up in front of the house, I parked and got out. I helped Sparkle out of the car and led her to the door. She was shocked when I opened the door and she noticed our place was already decked out wit' brand new furniture. I had hired an interior decorator to decorate and give it that special touch. I wanted shit to be right for Sparkle. I planned to prove to her that she was the only chick that I wanted and needed. Whatever it took to do it, I was down for it.

"Let me take you on a tour," I said to her after explaining that our new home had four bedrooms and four bathrooms. There was an extra large family room with a fireplace as soon as you walked in. Three more bedrooms were downstairs, and two out of the three had its own private bathroom area. The kitchen had two stoves, two dishwashers, a warming oven, and two sinks. The master bedroom was also huge and was equipped with a fireplace, but Sparkle was more in awe of the large master bathroom. It had two tubs; one was a Jacuzzi tub, and the other was an old fashioned tub with web feet. When I looked at the

Jacuzzi tub, I imagined us wrapped around each other in it making love. When I looked at the old fashioned tub I pictured her laying in it taking a long hot bubble bath, relaxing. There was also a shower big enough for four to six people. I mean, the realtor did her thang by finding me a fresh spot like this.

Outside there was an in ground storm shelter for protection during tornadoes and hurricanes. The garage was attached to the house as well as a heated and cooled workshop.

"I am in love with this place," Sparkle admitted wrapping her arms around my shoulders. "I can see us growing old together out here."

"Let's go back and freak in our new place."

She shook her head which kinda made me wonder what the fuck was wrong wit' her. My dick was harder than cement, and I needed to feel them guts. "I want you to have a check-up done first. I don't feel comfortable doin' that right now."

"Fuck you tryna say?"

"I'm not saying anything, but you gotta go and get yo' dipstick checked. I mean, I ain't the other broads, and I ain't letting you hit this raw until you do."

"So, it's like that?"

"Yep, that's how it is."

My third leg died and wasn't hard no mo'. I had to try to convince her to let me go up in that. Baby mama was always on some bullshit. I had done some questionable shit wit' Ginger and Jia, so I wasn't comfortable with the doctor's visit. I kno' they say it's better to kno' than not to. I figured we all had to die from somethin', but I wasn't wit' that shit right there.

The Results Could Be Deadly

Sparkle

The next morning I met up with Sayveon in the parking lot of a private health center off Woodrow Wilson Ave. We went in the building and signed in at the front desk. We sat down and waited like everyone else. As I sat there I thought to myself, I didn't have anything to be worried about, why am I so nervous.

"Sparkle Davis," a short, young, Caucasian woman called out. I followed her to the back where she led me into a small room. "I am the counselor, and I will explain to you the HIV testing procedure."

"Um hmm." My leg began to shake without me even noticing it until I looked down. I had been with Sayveon for many years, and he was my first sexual encounter. Ontavious was the only other man that I had ever slept with. I knew Sayveon had been a whore and fucked more bitches than the original Playboy, Hugh Hefner.

"We suggest that all of our clients use the oral HIV testing. The test doesn't use saliva. It uses a fluid called oral mucosal transudate, which lives in the cheeks and gums. We recommend this test because it's easy and quick and won't have to be sent to a laboratory. Would you agree to take this one?"

"Yes."

"I need you to sign this paper giving me consent to give you the test." She pushed a piece of paper to me and handed me an ink pen. I signed on the dotted line and pushed the paper back to the woman. She took me into another room, placed the end of the test strip in my mouth, and swabbed my cheek and gums. "I'm going to place this in a vial that holds an enzyme solution that reacts to any antibody-antigen binding. You can go back up front, and you'll be called with your results."

"Okay."

The next twenty minutes went by so slow. Sayveon had been called to the back as well and he had come back and plopped down beside me. We both were quiet as two church mice. Two more women came in and had gone to the back and were now seated and waiting too.

"Sparkle Davis." The lady called me once again. I knew that this time I would know the results. My heart began to thump hard, and my knees were getting weak. Once in the small room, one of the workers handed the counselor a folder and then left out.

The counselor opened the folder. From the look that she gave me, I knew that the news couldn't have been good. "

"I have your results, and you're HIV positive."

After hearing the diagnosis, I went numb. Everything suddenly went blank. I couldn't utter a word. The other woman quickly walked back in. "I'm so sorry. Give that folder back. Here is the right one."

She looked at me. My eyes were glossy and water was beginning to form. "Are you Sparkle Davis?"

"Yes."

"My apologies honey." She turned and exited the room.

The counselor opened up my folder. "Everything looks good, and you're negative."

I could breathe again. I wanted to scream, shout, and take off running. I held my head back and closed my eyes for a moment. I thought about what I would have done if I did have HIV. I came back to reality. "Y'all scared the hell out of me."

"I really apologize for that bit of confusion. I see so many girls come through, and they aren't nearly as fortunate as you were today. The results for them are that they have the disease. You're one of the lucky ones, Miss Davis." She smiled and patted my arm. "Are you okay after that shake up?"

"I guess."

"If you don't have any questions or concerns for me here is your copy of your results and you're welcomed to go."

"I don't have any questions. I'm good on that."

I didn't kno' whether to be mad at the hoe that brought in the wrong folder or jump for joy because I had a clean bill of health. I chose to let it go and focus on the good that came out of that scare. It made me realize how quickly my entire world could have turned upside down in a split second. Dang, I was satisfied that I had gotten a good report.

Got Me Sweatin'

Sayveon

All that shit 'bout taking that HIV test had me 'bout ready to start shittin' bricks. I played the cool, calm, and collected role, but deep down I had gotten anxious as a mothafucka! I replayed in my head all of the bitches I had smashed in the past. A few times I slipped and didn't strap up. I always figured that this day would catch up wit' me. The day I had to sit on edge wondering if a bitch had given me somethin' that I couldn't get rid of.

Sparkle was next to me, all cheerful and happy that she was straight and didn't have nothin'.

Damn, I wonder is Shameka still living. Or what 'bout that hoe named Tywanda? Then, I fucked that bad bitch Ashley back in the day, and I don't kno' if she's dead or alive. Fuck! I gotta stop stressin' before I give myself a heart attack! I thought to myself as I waited to be called.

"Sayveon Travis," the woman said out loud when she appeared from the back area.

I stood and followed her to the back. She led me into a room and told me to have a seat. She opened up the folder. "You're perfectly healthy. You came back HIV negative."

I let out a slow sigh. "Good."

"Would you like to ask me anything?"

"Nope. It's good on my end."

"Well here is a copy of your results, and you're free to leave. Please keep being safe," she advised.

"A'ight."

On our way out, I couldn't help but appreciate my woman more. Only a real woman would demand her man get an HIV test and take one with him. It showed how much she loved herself and me and that she wasn't willing to jeopardize either of our lives. If she hadn't insisted on taking the test I would never know my status. Sparkle had always been a rider and held me down. I wasn't in my feelings no more 'bout her walking away and ending thangs the first time. I had shitted on her way too many times. I pushed my selfishness aside and looked at it from her point of view. She had stood by me and didn't dip out at the first sign of stormy weather. In the past she had rode wit' me through any and er'thang, and soon it started to become foolish. She had to draw the line somewhere. I respected her decision to demand respect from a nigga. She could now rock her title of my 'wifey' like it was a badge of honor.

I kissed her on the jaw and whispered, "You're my ride or die chick, huh?"

She stopped dead in her tracks. "Let me explain something to you that I've learned from us not being together." She looked up at me with sincerity and added, "I no longer wanna be labeled as that. Sticking by my man through hard times is one thing. Allowing a man to make a fool of me is something else. To be a woman that stands by her man is commendable; to be a ride or die is stupid and foolish. Sometimes staying isn't what makes you strong. Knowing your worth and deciding not to tolerate disrespect is even stronger. I understand that people make mistakes but once it becomes a habit, it's time to move on."

"I feel you, baby. I'm ready to show you that I'm keepin' it one thousand 'dis' time. No games and no other women. Stop thinkin' I'm tryna play you and trust me. I got you."

She rested her head on my chest, and deep down I felt that my girl and I would be a'ight. It seemed as though I was starting to get my family back.

Long Time Coming

Sparkle

I took a hold of Sayveon's dick and straddled him, guiding him into my soft wet hole. He pushed against me, and I moaned when I felt his touch. When he slid into me, the sensation made my toes curl. I held on to his wrists and arched my back as we fucked. He opened his eyes and saw that I was watching him, my mouth wide open and eyes half closed in lust. His gaze explored my chocolately skin. He was buried so deep inside of me, and it felt so good.

I increased my pace as I used my fingers to grip his wrists. My moans came out low at first and then got louder with each thrust. I worked my hips on top of him and my breathing became rough as he rocked his body back in rhythm with mine. I leaned over and pressed my forehead to his, and my hips bucked wildly. My nails dug into his skin. My movements increased even more. I threw my head back and let out a scream from the back of my throat. I buried my face under his jaw.

"Certified A-1 pussy," he said as he held on to my hips.

I groaned against Sayveon's neck and clamped my hips down on him. I lifted myself up off his chest as my legs began shuddering, and I creamed all over his long stick. I screamed and threw myself forward on him, sinking my teeth into his chest.

I rolled off of Sayveon and collapsed on the bed. He re-opened my legs and dived inside of me. His thrust became harder and harder until he shot off. I let out a deep breath. He laid right beside me and let me rest in his arms.

"I love you," his deep voice said.

"I love you, too. I always have and always will."

The spark in our relationship had been rekindled, and I was loving every bit of it.

When Sayveon went to the shower, his cell phone rang. I reached over and grabbed it from the nightstand. The caller was someone named 'Sunshine.' I knew this mothafucka couldn't be trusted! Instead of arguing with one of those random bitches, I tossed his phone back on the table. It then beeped alerting that a text message had come through. I decided to pick the phone back up and check the message. It read: Well, congrats on your engagement and I wish you and the lucky lady the very best. I won't bother you again. Take care of yourself and your new fiancé!

I called the number back to find out what was really going on with the two of them.

"What's up, Sayveon?" the light voiced woman answered.

"I'm his fiancé Sparkle."

"Oh, well hi."

I didn't speak back, and the phone was silent for a minute. "Who are you is what I'm trying to find out."

"I'm an old friend. We spoke back and forth last night through text. His last message to me was that he had gotten engaged. I'm just seeing it for some strange reason, and I only wanted to tell him congratulations."

"I'll be sure to tell him what you said."

"Toodles," she said and ended the call.

I was more at ease after hearing what the 'Sunshine' chick had to say. My trust needed to be combined with the willingness to forgive him for all of the shit that he had done. That's exactly what I planned to do. He was changing, and I was sure that it wouldn't happen overnight, but at least he was trying to do better. He was starting to prove to me that it was possible to rebuild trust in someone who had greatly disappointed me. I'd give it a li'l more time before I completely dropped my guards, but he was making some good progress. I couldn't have asked for more.

Our Lovely Day

Sparkle

Three months later, Sayveon and I had our outdoor wedding. It was warm, but not terribly so. The May sun peeped out occasionally. A pleasant breeze rustled the surrounding shrubs in our backyard, cooling the guests and family members. They took their seats on either side of the aisle leading to the altar. Sweet strains of music drifted through the crowd. I couldn't believe it; I was marrying my best friend, homey, and the father of my child. It would be a memorable day for us both.

The music stopped, and all heads turned. The singer Mul-Ty began to sing 'Looking For Love.' He held the microphone. "See I/ been looking for love/ and I found it in you/ my dream come true…" I walked down the aisle wearing a beautiful white fitted gown. On my head was a two-tier veil with a matching crystal headpiece. I held a French rose silk bouquet. My cousin Deuce held my arm as we reached the altar. There awaiting me was the pastor and my husband-to-be. Sayveon looked so handsome. He wore a black, single breasted, satin tuxedo with a white-wing collar shirt.

The music soon faded, and the pastor stepped to the mic, Bible in hand. He smiled at the assembly. "Cherished family members and honored guests, I would like to thank each of you for coming out this evening," he said. The sound carried well from the small speakers to either side of the podium. The pastor placed the Bible down before him. "Let us begin by offering thanks to the Lord on this wonderful day." We all bowed our heads and he prayed.

After the prayer was over, the preacher led us through our vows. It was now time for the exchange of rings. Menace's adorable li'l son dressed in a white tuxedo walked up and handed Sayveon a ring. He slipped it on my finger. I soon was given the opportunity to place his on his finger as well. "By the power vested unto me I now proclaim you husband and wife. You may now kiss the bride." Sayveon placed his hands on my shoulders and did so.

The pastor held up his hands, bringing the crowd to their feet. My husband and I walked down the aisle, arms linked with identical smiles on our faces. The best man who was Pops, Mama V who was my maid of honor, the groomsmen, and bridesmaids followed behind us. They stopped near the end of the walk, forming the start of the receiving line. The family and guests filed down, pausing for hugs and kisses and congratulating us.

Right when we were about to take off, I spotted Mrs. Travis standing there with Aunt Ruby. Mrs. Travis held Layla on her hip. Our daughter looked like a doll in her all white dress with cute white ribbons in her hair. Sayveon and I both kissed our baby and then ran to the long white limo that waited for us. Sayveon tried his best not to step on my long dress train that dragged the ground. The ribbons, twisted coils, and streamers whisked in the wind behind us as we headed to the reception. Our wedding had turned out to be a beautiful and delightful ceremony. I had the wedding that I had always dreamed of with the man who I always loved.

Out Of Nowhere

Sparkle

Over a hundred guests showed up at our wedding reception. Everything was perfect from our lovely floral arrangements to the four-layered white cake. There was enough food to feed an army and still have plenty left over. I enjoyed the dancing and conversing with family and friends. But of course as we all know, all good things have to end. I then turned around and tossed my bouquet behind me. The women collided with each other as they tried to catch it. The lucky lady who held it in her grasp was Mama V. Sayveon and I said our goodbyes to everyone, and we left the reception to head to the honeymoon.

Sayveon had gone back to our home, gotten his ride, and gotten our luggage. "So, baby, where are we going now?" I asked as we walked to the car with family and friends following behind us. He wanted our honeymoon destination to be a surprise and had kept it from me.

"Turtle Bay Resort in Hawaii."

"Oh, baby! We're gonna have some fun." I rubbed my belly. "We might luck up and make another one."

He looked over and smiled. "You better be careful what you ask for, girl. You just might get it."

I laughed as we got in the car at the same time. I buckled my seatbelt, and he was about to pull off when Menace, Bone, and Vicious came up to the car in their tuxedos looking like they had a bit too much to drink. Menace said, "Sparkle, you're all the way in the fam now, and we welcome you."

"Awl, how sweet and thank you."

"A'ight, Cuzzo we'll holla," Sayveon said as we pulled off.

When we got back home, Sayveon told me to go on and get our things together and that he would be right back. "I ain't got no weed, and I gotta smoke before we get on that plane later on. Gotta keep calm."

He dropped me off in the yard and let the window down. "Do you want me to wait for you to go on in?" he wanted to know.

"I'm good. You can go on." It was almost dark, but I could still see. I was just so gassed up because we were about to go somewhere that I had never been. In my mind I could see the water crashing against the huge stones. Being in Hawaii would feel like heaven to an angel.

When I made it to the front step, I was suddenly thrown down onto the ground and my wrists were pinned to my sides. I tried to scream, but the stranger's mouth was on mine. I turned my face away, but he used one hand to force my mouth in his direction. The other hand was squeezing both of my wrists. I twisted and turned my head until I was able to let out a loud yell. He quickly covered my yells with his hand and then slapped me across the face.

His heavy body laid on mine and no matter how hard I tried to push him off, I couldn't.

I looked at him wondering if I knew him but I didn't. He was a white guy in his mid thirties with jet-black hair and devilish green eyes. He used all of his strength to tear open my wedding gown and expose my breasts . He acted like a crazed animal as he licked up and down my nipples. I felt the tears roll down my face when he unzipped his blue- jeans. I began to squirm and kick. Nothing would stop him. I dug my fingernails as hard as I could into his back until I felt the blood leak out. He continued to try to rape me as if he didn't feel shit.

Somehow he found a way to get out of his boxers. My underwear had been torn and he tried to push himself inside of me but I kept my legs shut tight. I screamed and screamed through his muffled hand and forced my knees to stay together. He pulled out a knife and ran the blade over my neck just hard enough to draw blood. Seeing the knife and feeling the blood trickle made me quiet. I knew that he meant business then.

"I'll kill you," he breathed into me.

I wanted to holler out again but the cold blade kept me quiet. Right when he stuck his dick on my vagina we heard a vehicle coming up the street. Sayveon whipped into the driveway with his bright lights shining on us. The man jumped up bouncing on one leg trying to get his pants up. Sayveon shot out of his ride with his weapon in his hand and let off several rounds. The first bullet missed the guy but the second one hit him. The man held on to his side and fell down. I hopped up from where I laid and ran over to Sayveon and the dude on the ground gasping for air.

"Please, don't kill me, man," he pleaded.

"Who the fuck are you, mothafucka?" Sayveon roared standing on top of him.

"I was sent by Ginger," he quickly revealed. "She hired me to keep tabs on you. She told me that you two weren't going to be here, you're supposed to be on your honeymoon."

"Who told her about that?"

"I don't know."

Sayveon's and my eyes widened. "Well, how the fuck would she have known it?" Sayveon asked, fishing for more information.

"I have no idea, but it's more than likely someone in your circle. Look, I'm just trying to live. All I ask is that you spare me."

Sayveon aimed the burner at the dude's head and squeezed the trigger. The man's eyes rolled back in his head, and his mouth was left opened wide. He shook a few times before he completely stopped breathing. Sayveon's eyes told me that he was furious.

"I'ma kill that bitch!" he snarled.

I knew that he meant every word of what he had spoken. Now I had to watch my back because of the crazed bitch Ginger, but this was only the beginning of the beef that the two of them would have. He would eventually see how burning bridges could get you fucked up. His pain would turn into ongoing drama that seemed like it would never end. On down the line, the snakes in his circle would be shown up one by one.

To Be Continued...

Made in United States
North Haven, CT
01 February 2022